KARIN TIDBECK

AMATKA

Karin Tidbeck is originally from Stockholm, Sweden. She lives and works in Malmö as a freelance writer, translator, and creative-writing teacher and writes fiction in Swedish and English. She debuted in 2010 with the Swedish short story collection *Vem är Arvid Pekon?* Her English debut, the 2012 collection *Jagannath*, was awarded the Crawford Award in 2013 and shortlisted for the World Fantasy Award. *Amatka* is her first novel.

ALSO BY KARIN TIDBECK

Jagannath

AMATKA

AMATKA

KARIN TIDBECK

VINTAGE BOOKS
A Division of Penguin Random House LLC
New York

A VINTAGE BOOKS ORIGINAL, JUNE 2017

English translation copyright © 2017 by Karin Tidbeck

All rights reserved. Published in the United States by Vintage Books, a division of Penguin Random House LLC, New York, and distributed in Canada by Random House of Canada, a division of Penguin Random House Canada Limited, Toronto. Originally published in Sweden by Mix Förlag, Stockholm, in 2012. Copyright © 2012 by Karin Tidbeck.

Vintage and colophon are registered trademarks of Penguin Random House LLC.

Library of Congress Cataloging-in-Publication Data
Names: Tidbeck, Karin, 1977– author.
Title: Amatka / Karin Tidbeck.
Other titles: Amatka. English
Description: New York : Vintage, 2017.
Identifiers: LCCN 2016043285 (print) | LCCN 2017002988 (ebook) |
ISBN 9781101973950 (paperback) | ISBN 9781101973967 (ebook)
Subjects: LCSH: Language and languages—Fiction. | BISAC: FICTION /
Literary. | FICTION / Science Fiction / General. | FICTION /
Visionary & Metaphysical. | GSAFD: Dystopian fiction.
Classification: LCC PT9877.3.I45 A6313 2017 (print) | LCC PT9877.3.I45
(ebook) | DDC 839.73/8—dc23
LC record available at https://lccn.loc.gov/2016043285

Vintage Books Trade Paperback ISBN: 978-1-101-97395-0
eBook ISBN: 978-1-101-97396-7

Book design by Anna B. Knighton

Printed in the United States of America
10 9 8 7 6 5 4 3 2 1

AMATKA

THE TRAIN

Brilars' Vanja Essre Two, information assistant with the Essre Hygiene Specialists, was the only passenger on the auto train bound for Amatka. As soon as she had climbed the steps, the door shut behind her and the train jerked into motion. Vanja took a new grip on her satchel and typewriter case and pushed the suitcase through the sliding door with her feet. On the other side, the darkness was complete. She fumbled along the wall and found a circuit breaker next to the door. The light that flickered on was weak and yellow.

The narrow space of the passenger car was bare except for the brown vinyl bunk couches that lined the walls and the luggage racks, stacked with blankets and thin pillows, which were wide enough to sleep on, too. It was built for migration, for transporting pioneers to new frontiers, and its capacity was pointless here.

Vanja left her bags by the door and sat on each of the couches. They were all equally rigid and uncomfortable. The upholstery looked slippery but felt unpleasantly rough to the touch. She chose the couch at the far right-hand corner, where she'd be close to the common room and have a good view of the rest of the car. It was all vaguely reminiscent of the dormitory in Children's House Two so long ago: the same vinyl mattresses under the sheets, the same lingering scent of bodies. But back then the room had been full of children and the sound of their voices.

She took a look at the tiny common room. The only window in the car was on the right wall, low and wide with rounded edges and a roll-down curtain. On closer inspection, the window turned out not to be an ordinary window, but a white screen that lit up at the press of a button. It was probably meant as a substitute for daylight. Under the screen, a table was bolted to the floor along with four chairs. One of the two high cabinets on the other side of the room held a tiny lavatory with a washbasin, the other a small pantry with preserves and fresh root vegetables. Everything was marked in large and comforting letters: WASHBASIN, PANTRY, TABLE. This area smelled vaguely of manure, either from the lavatory or from the containers that rode at the front of the train.

Vanja fetched her suitcase and undid the buckles. One of them looked like it was about to come loose. It had been a gift from someone, who had inherited it from someone else, and so on. In any case, it wasn't going to last long: the word SUITCASE was almost illegible. She could fill in the letters, of course, but the question was what would happen first—that the bag simply fell apart from wear or that it dissolved when she put it away. She really ought to scrap it.

"Suitcase," Vanja whispered, to keep it its shape just a little longer. "Suitcase, suitcase."

She flipped the backrest to free up the lower bunk and made the bed with the set of sheets she'd brought. They too would soon need new marking.

The preserves in the pantry were apparently meant to be eaten cold. Vanja found a spoon and pulled the lid off one of the cans. According to the ingredient list, it contained "stew with a base of mycoprotein," which meant a smooth, bland paste that stuck to the roof of her mouth. Vanja forced down half of the can's contents and put it back in the pantry. The vegetables were fresh and tasted better. She cut a chunk of rutabaga into smaller pieces and slowly ate them one by one.

The train car swayed gently back and forth; a rhythmic pounding noise emerged through the floor, and though this must mean that the train was moving forward, it was impossible to tell at what speed. The window screen grew dim. Vanja looked at the clock on her wrist. The second indicator was stuck at one o'clock, twitching. She had forgotten to follow instructions; she should have left it at home or handed it in at the station. Looking at it while on the train was a bad idea. Unless they were made from fine matter, mechanical things sometimes didn't behave like they should between the colonies. The train was safe, of course, but the little clock might not be. Vanja took it off and put it in her pocket.

She went back into the main car and changed into sleep clothes. They were getting too big for her, again. Her breasts dangled half-empty on her ribs; her belly no longer sagged from fat but from loose skin and flaccid musculature; her legs were no longer firm. She knew her face had thinned down in the same doughy manner, its warm bronze yellowed and fading into the shade of her dull eyes and hair in a nondescript spectrum of brown. She looked older than she was. Her supervisor, Illas' Öydis, had treated her with exaggerated care. This is an important mission, she had said, so take all the time you need. No need to hurry. It was an important mission, carried out with the committee's blessing. She was, after all, the first of her kind.

Vanja left the ceiling light on and huddled under the blanket. Everyone knew that there was nothing out there except the empty steppe: billowing grass, some hillocks, and combes. The lack of windows was just a security measure. She tried to give in to the rocking of the train. The corner should have felt safe, but it didn't. The walls were too thin, a frail shell between her and the unseen landscape through which she was traveling.

THE FIRST WEEK

FIRSTDAY

Vanja watched from the doorway as the train pulled in to Amatka's station, a simple block of concrete in the colony's outer ring. The colony looked small compared to Essre, but its shape was familiar: the low gray cubes and rectangles of houses placed in concentric rings around the central building, the eight streets radiating from its center to the outer ring of domed plant houses. Beyond them, the yellowy gray of the endless tundra.

She heaved her suitcase down onto the platform, where it landed with a thud. She stepped off the train and shuddered. The air was raw, noticeably colder than in Essre. A group of workers waited on the platform to unload the two freight cars attached to the end of the train and load the pallets and sacks that stood in neat rows on the concrete.

A woman in blue overalls and jacket approached along the platform. Wisps of auburn hair curled out from under her black hat. She was maybe half a head taller than Vanja, possibly the same age as her, green-eyed.

"Welcome to Amatka. Ulltors' Nina Four." Her smile revealed a small gap between her front teeth.

Vanja took her outstretched hand. "Brilars' Vanja Essre Two."

A nauseating stink was spreading across the platform. The workers had begun to unload the large manure barrels from one of the freight cars.

Nina followed Vanja's gaze. "It's for the mushroom farms. You send us shit and get mushrooms back. Practical, isn't it?" She chuckled.

"Oh. Yes." Vanja cleared her throat.

Nina smiled. "Come on, let's go. It's not far." She picked the suitcase up one-handed. "You'll meet the others at home."

Nina kept talking as they left the platform and walked toward the center of the colony. She was excited to have a lodger, she said; it was the first time her household had been drawn in the solidarity lottery. And since Amatka got so few visitors, it was a special occasion. Vanja refrained from impolitely asking how the household members would be compensated, but Nina told her anyway: they would be allowed time off.

"And it's great that you gave such early notice," she added. "This way we had time to get your room ready."

Vanja blinked. "A whole room? Why?"

Nina shrugged. "It's been empty for a while. Olof, the guy who lived there before, moved out last year."

"In Essre, we're two to a room. Even three, sometimes."

"We've been short on people for a while."

"Short? I've never heard of a shortage before. Why is that?"

Nina briefly clenched her jaw before giving what sounded like a rehearsed reply. "There was an accident. We lost a hundred comrades. It's been a while, we're recovering, and the committee has decided that we don't talk about it. I'm only telling you this so you'll know. And that's all there is to say about it."

Nina paused. "Textile workshop," she said, and pointed at the building nearest to them.

"Textile workshop," Vanja repeated automatically.

They'd already passed the plant houses and entered the factory ring, which consisted of gently curved one-floor buildings with small windows and wide doors. Their facades were all marked with name and function in black, square letters. "Vegetable refinery," Nina continued, pointing at the next building.

"Vegetable refinery."

"Medical supplies factory." It was slightly smaller than the others.

"Medical supplies factory."

Repair workshop, printing workshop, paper factory. Nina pointed out each one, naming them in turn, and Vanja repeated her words. The factories were smaller than in Essre but seemed to be better maintained. The words painted on them looked wet and fresh.

The streets were all but empty. The few people who passed by walked with hurried steps, and Nina's voice echoed alone. Vanja stopped and dug her wrist clock out of her pocket.

"What time is it?"

"Ten thirty."

The clock still worked. It was, however, running either six hours slow or fast. Vanja set it and struggled to put it on, her fingers cold and clumsy. She pulled her sleeves down over her hands and picked the typewriter case up.

They left the factories and entered the residential ring, where narrow alleys separated three-story houses. Through a window in the nearest building, Vanja glimpsed two men by the kitchen sink, one washing dishes and the other drying them.

Nina pointed. "Kitchens are on the ground floor, as you can see, and bathrooms, too. The two upper floors have three rooms each."

Vanja nodded. "Kitchen and bathroom on the ground floor, three rooms each on the upper floors."

"On the two upper floors," Nina corrected.

"Sorry. On the two upper floors. I didn't sleep very well on the train."

Nina gave her a pat on the shoulder and pointed to the long children's house that could be glimpsed farther down the curve of the residential ring. They continued inward to the first ring. A full quarter of its circumference was taken up by the clinic that dwarfed the other facilities. And in the very center, a towering pillar that Nina didn't need to mention. Vanja knew exactly what it was: the commune office.

Nina pointed out the stores—pharmacy, groceries, clothing, tools, household items, sundries.

"You did bring your credit book, didn't you?"

Vanja pulled out the little green booklet from the breast pocket of her anorak. It was made of good paper, recycled cellulose from the old world. Personal documents were too valuable to use mere mycopaper. "I got an advance on next month's credit. And a special one for requisitions."

"For what?"

"I mean the company's requisitions. So I can collect things for the study. For my assignment."

Nina scratched her chin. "You know, we weren't actually told what it is you'll be doing here."

"I'm an information assistant." Vanja tucked the booklet away. "I'm supposed to find out what kind of hygiene products people use here. Soap and such. So the company knows what products they should try to launch here."

Nina hummed. "I suppose it's mostly the commune's own products. I don't know what it's like in Essre, but nothing much changed here after they allowed free production. People around here, they like familiar things. But why did you have to come all the way out here to find that out? Don't you know all about these things in Essre already?"

Vanja shook her head. "The administration does, I guess. But it takes so long to get the facts; it's forms here and forms there. There are so many new companies now. And my supervisor wanted more than just figures. She wants to know what people want. So here I am."

"How many of you are there in this . . ."

"The Essre Hygiene Specialists," Vanja said.

"You can just call it E.H.S."

"How many employees are you at E.H.S.?"

"Twenty, but I am the first to venture out of Essre as part of this new program."

"Wow," said Nina. "And you're going to make us use our credit to buy your soap."

"Yes."

"Why? I mean, what difference does it make?"

"I don't know," Vanja replied. "Because it's new."

"I don't know if I think that's a good thing," Nina said. "We're here."

They'd made their way through the center and arrived at the residential houses on the other side. Nina turned down the row and opened the third door on the right, marked HOUSEHOLD NUMBER 24. She set the suitcase down in the little hallway and opened the door to the kitchen.

The ground-floor kitchen and common room was sparsely furnished and had only two small windows. Under the one facing the street was a stove and a kitchen counter with shelves and an inlaid sink. A small refrigerator rattled in the corner. Cans and carefully sealed bags were lined up in neat rows on the shelves of the doorless pantry next to the fridge. Everything looked old and worn but carefully marked. Vanja thought of her own kitchen, where the labels were scratched and worn: not so here. The long dining table against the far wall was covered by a bright yellow cloth that was almost luminous in the drabness.

A slender man with his plaid shirt stuffed into a pair of green dungarees stood by the sink with a steaming cup in his hand. He put it down and came to greet Vanja.

"This is Jonids' Ivar," said Nina. "Ivar, Brilars' Vanja."

"Welcome." Ivar's handshake was dry and light. He briefly met Vanja's eyes before looking away. His dark eyes were bloodshot. "Hello. And good-bye. I'm off to my shift."

He stepped past Nina, who stroked his back, and into the hallway.

"So that was Ivar," Nina said when he'd closed the door behind him. "He works at the mushroom farms. He's really very sweet. He's just a little terse."

"Don't you have to go to work?"

"I've got the day off. So if you want me to take you anywhere or something, just ask. Otherwise I'll probably be reading in my room."

Nina gave her a tour of the kitchen, which looked just like the one at home. Everyone took turns buying food according to a shopping list displayed on the fridge door. Behind the kitchen there was a bathroom. Then Nina guided Vanja back into the hallway and up the narrow stairs to the apartments. The door on the first landing had only one name on it: DOOR. HERE LIVES SAROLS' ULLA THREE.

"That's where Ulla lives," said Nina. "She used to be a doctor."

"She has this floor all to herself?"

"I suppose you think that's strange, but yes, she does."

Vanja shuddered. "I see."

"We check in on her every day, go around the rooms and mark everything. You're very welcome to help. She's getting a little senile, but she means well." Nina continued up the next flight of stairs. "The alternative is to leave some houses empty, Vanja."

Vanja's room was of standard size but furnished for one person instead of two. The bed by the far wall had a thick mattress and ample storage space under its high frame; a quilted duvet, a worn blanket, and a pillow lay neatly stacked at the foot of the bed. By the window a small desk and a chair had replaced the usual second bed, but there were still two storage cabinets that Vanja would have all to herself.

Nina set the bag down on the bed. "I'll let you make yourself at home." She went into her own room next door.

Vanja put her satchel and typewriter case down in the doorway and made a circuit of the room. She touched each object, reading its label and saying its name aloud. When she was done, she heaved the heavy typewriter case onto the desk and stacked the satchel's contents—folders, typewriter paper, and notepads—next to it.

Finally, she emptied her suitcase: the set of sheets, which she laid out on the mattress; towels, sleep clothes, a few sets of underwear, trousers, sweaters, and a pair of overalls, all of which she folded and put in one of the cabinets. The suitcase only just fit under the bed. After some consideration she put on another pair of trousers and the thickest sweater she'd brought. It didn't make her feel much warmer.

"You need proper clothes." Nina was back, leaning against the door frame.

Vanja pulled the sweater down over her hips. The shirt underneath bunched up. "You're right. But I'm not sure what I need. Is it always this cold?"

"Yep."

"Do you get used to it?"

Nina grinned and shook her head. "Nope. But you'll get very good at dressing for the weather." She pulled away from the door frame and went back into her own room.

Vanja sat down at the desk, took the lid off the typewriter case, and loaded a blank sheet. After punching the buttons one by one, reciting each character and number, she was confident everything was in working order.

There was a knock on the open door, and Nina entered with a note in her hand.

"Here," she said. "I've made a list of the clothes we wear here. So you know what to get."

Vanja scanned the list. "A sleeping cap?"

"The nights are even colder."

Vanja thanked her and turned back to the desk to organize her papers. After a while she fetched the blanket from the bed and wrapped herself in it until only her head and hands could be seen. The temperature in the house wasn't much higher than outside.

Her assignment was to find out everything E.H.S. needed to know about hygiene habits and needs in Amatka. That was it. Vanja had asked for more details, but Öydis, the supervisor, had shrugged her shoulders.

"We've never done this before, Vanja. Nobody's done it before. We're pioneers, you know? Just like our forebears. You, Vanja, have the honor of being a pioneer in this project. You're perfectly suited. I'm sure you'll find a good solution."

Vanja still didn't fully understand why she was so perfect for the job. Öydis had referred to her "quiet discretion." Vanja suspected, however, that it had more to do with Ärna's powers of persuasion. Ärna had told her she ought to have a change of scenery, and then made it happen. She was ever the big sister. Nepotism wasn't really allowed, but Ärna had risen quickly through the ranks at E.H.S. and somehow managed to get Vanja the position.

She put two folders on the desk in front of her and took a thick marking pen from her satchel. She marked one folder CONTENTS: REPORTS and the other CONTENTS: NOTES. She picked up the notepad and leafed through it. It was mycopaper, shiny and new, with the scrap-by date printed in the bottom right corner of every single sheet. There should be time enough to fill the whole notepad, and transcribe the important parts, before it had to be scrapped.

Vanja was supposed to submit reports once a week. She grabbed a pencil and stepped out into the hallway to knock on Nina's door.

Report 1

The following notes are the result of my first meeting with one of my hosts, Ulltors' Nina Amatka Four.

The household consists of three people: Nina, Jonids' Ivar Four (farming technician), and Sarols' Ulla Three (retired physician). Nina is 34 years old and employed as a medic at Amatka's clinic. She informs me that Ivar is 32 years old and employed as a farming technician in the mushroom farming chambers. Both were reared in Children's House Four in Amatka. They have produced two children together, Ninivs' Tora Four and Ninivs' Ida Four, eight and six years old respectively. The girls live in Children's House Four and visit during weekends.

The general attitude to hygiene in Amatka is somewhat different, chiefly on account of the cold and the conditions it entails. Each household is allotted a ration of hot water, which is rarely enough to fill more than one bathtub. For this reason, household comrades often coordinate bathing. Nina states that the members of this household bathe every week to ten days. Otherwise they use washcloths to wash. Nina also informs me that the soap they normally use is difficult to rinse off with water and washcloth alone.

When it comes to hygiene products, the household uses the commune's standard products without exception. Nina appears negatively inclined to externally sourced products. Her opinion is that it is important to maintain a basic standard, but she declines expanding further on the subject.

SECONDAY

Vanja woke to the sound of thunder. The little windowpane showed a brightening sky, halfway between black and the gray of the daylight hours. She waited for the patter of rain against the glass. Nothing happened. Instead, more thunder.

She had gone to bed early, shortly after dinner. They'd had boiled turnips and carrots with savory fried mushrooms, a small round variety Vanja had never seen before. Ulla, who turned out to be old and bent but with a sharp gaze, had joined them at the table. She asked countless questions about Essre: how many people lived there nowadays, what did they wear, who was on the committee, and above all—was free production really a good idea? It seemed that the general population of Amatka didn't receive much news from the rest of the colonies.

Vanja replied as well as she could. The last question she had no answer for, other than the official statement: to stimulate the people's pioneering spirit and encourage cooperative development. It's just my job, she'd said, I do what they tell me. Ulla shook her head and wondered how Vanja could be so uninterested. You're completely inane, she'd said, and Vanja stared down at her plate. Nina had told Ulla that she ought to think before she spoke. Ulla had replied that she was too old for that.

Vanja excused herself, washed her plate and cutlery, and retired to her room, where she got into bed with her clothes on. No one came after her. It seemed that a closed door was respected in Amatka, too. She had lain awake for a long time, sorting through the things that had been said and done, coming up with all kinds of caustic retorts she could have delivered. Essre and its committee were ambitious and thinking ahead; free production was a necessary step in the expansion of the colonies. The people were ready to give it a try, in a carefully controlled effort. Amatka seemed to be doing well, no matter what Ulla might think. Did Ulla not have faith in her comrades?

Her boots lay next to the bed; she'd managed to take those off, at least. She pushed the duvet aside and shuddered in the sudden cold. She fumbled her shoes on, fetched a towel and washcloth from the cabinet, and went downstairs.

Ivar was at the kitchen table, eating with an opened book on the table in front of him. He nodded at her and jerked his thumb at the frying pan and the steaming pot sitting on the stove. Vanja nodded in reply and went into the bathroom. There was just enough room for a toilet bowl, sink, and bathtub. The third shelf on the wall was hers, not that she owned anything other than some washing products and a toothbrush. She reached for her toiletry bag, mumbled "toiletry bag," and opened it.

She twitched and almost dropped the bag in the sink when she saw the contents. The bottom of the bag was coated in a thick paste. It was the toothbrush. She'd been careless. She'd noticed it on the train: the letters TOOTHBRUSH etched into the shaft had begun to lose their definition. Still, she'd thought it would last a little while longer.

Vanja forced herself to close the zipper. Now that she knew what was inside, holding it made her fingers tingle. She had a sudden vision of the contents escaping, slithering up her arms. The thought made her throat burn. She backed out of the bathroom with the toiletry bag in both hands.

"Ivar?"

Ivar's hand and fork stopped midway between the plate and his mouth. "Yes?"

"I need to scrap this." She turned around to show him the bag.

Ivar looked at what was in her hands, then at her, and nodded curtly. He rose from the table, went over to a cabinet under the sink, and pulled out a box. He opened the lid and held the box out to Vanja, who carefully placed the toiletry bag on the bottom. Then he put the lid back on and left. Vanja heard the front door open and close. Ivar came back in and sat down at the table.

"I apologize," Vanja said.

Ivar smiled at her for the first time, a small smile with lips closed, and his face softened. "Don't worry about it. Make sure you eat something." He returned to his book.

Vanja fetched a cup and a plate and looked out the window. It still wasn't raining. In the frying pan she found reheated leftovers from yesterday's dinner; the pot contained coffee, so strong it was nearly brown. Vanja let the grounds sink and tasted it. It tasted unfamiliar, spicy and both sour and sweet, made from some mushroom unknown in Essre. She filled her plate and sat down across from Ivar. From what she could make out of the upside-down text, he was reading about plant-house farming.

When Ivar had emptied his plate, he stood up and closed the book.

"I'm off to my shift now," he said. "Nina's already at hers. She started early. You're on cooking duty tonight. But you don't have to get anything from the store. There's plenty in the pantry."

Vanja nodded. "What time?"

Ivar shrugged. "We'll be home around five." Saying nothing more, he washed his plate and left.

"Let's mark all the things in here," Vanja sang under her breath, letting her eyes wander around the room. "Table, chair, and a pot here; stovetop, fridge, and pantry there. We mark all things in our care."

"The Marking Song" was part of everyone's life, from the first day at the children's house. When Vanja was younger, marking day at the children's house was the best day of the week.

Her teacher Jonas would walk around the room, pointing at objects one after the other. Sometimes it was hard to make the name of a thing fit the rhythm of the song, and they laughed. Vanja's voice was the loudest. Then they'd sing "The Pioneer Song" and "When I Grow Up." Afterward it was nap time.

It was not until much later that they were told the reason for all this marking and naming. It was a special lesson. The children had spent several days before this lesson retouching signs and labels, singing extra rounds of marking songs. Teacher Jonas monitored them closely, punishing the careless. Finally, the children gathered in the classroom. The lecture was short. Teacher Jonas stood at the desk, his face tense and grim. In a silence so complete one could hear one's own pulse, Jonas spoke. His powerful voice sounded thin.

A long time ago, when the pioneers came here, they built five colonies. Now only four remain.

When the lesson was over, the children spent the rest of the day singing marking songs and retouching signs and labels with a new intensity. It wasn't a game anymore.

Vanja had been in a storeroom, tasked with marking pencils and rulers, and she took to the job in earnest. *Pencil pencil pencil pencil pencil pencil*, she had chanted, touching the pencils one by one, until the stream of words inverted and made a sound like *cil-pen cil-pen cil-pen cil-pen cil-pen cil-pen*, and the row of pencils had shuddered and almost turned into something else, and she realized that this is how it happens, and her whole chest tingled. Right then, the door to the storeroom opened, and Teacher Jonas was in the doorway. He looked at the row of pencils, then at Vanja. "I saw that," he said. Then he grabbed her by the arm and steered her into the classroom.

The other children were already in their seats, except for Ärna, who was standing at the teacher's desk with a strange expression on her face. Teacher Jonas pushed Vanja ahead of him and made her stand next to her sister. Vanja looked down at her shoes and waited. He was going to tell the others what he had seen, and she would be sent away. The silence seemed endless. She was about to look up when teacher Jonas spoke. "Vanja and Ärna's father, Anvars' Lars, has been taken into custody on charges of subversive activity."

A murmur rippled through the classroom. "We have just talked about Colony Five and what happens when rules are broken. Now you all understand just what a terrible thing that is. A truly terrible, terrible thing. Do you want to destroy our community, to ruin everything we've struggled so hard to build?"

He turned to Vanja and Ärna. Vanja's head filled with a buzzing noise. His voice seemed remote. "It's important that you girls renounce your father and his actions. Because you don't want to be traitors like him, do you?"

"No." That was Ärna.

"Then say after me: 'As a loyal comrade of the commune, I renounce Anvars' Lars and his actions.'"

Ärna repeated his words, her voice so bright and loud Vanja could hear it through the growing roar in her ears. Vanja had to be guided through the sentence word for word, three times until Teacher Jonas was satisfied. Then they were allowed to return to their seats.

Teacher Jonas held a speech about the importance of reporting infractions immediately and renouncing anyone who tried to bring harm to the commune. After class, teacher Jonas took Vanja to see a committee official.

Teacher Jonas told us about what happened with the pencils, the official said. *You're just a child. You didn't know that what you did was wrong. Now you know better.*

Yes, Vanja had replied, eyes downcast. *I know better now.*

We will be watching you, the official said.

It was time for Vanja to register at the commune office in Amatka. She left the house dressed in two pairs of trousers, with three sweaters under her anorak and her notebooks in her satchel. She pulled down the anorak sleeves over her hands. The sky had brightened to a light shade of gray. Farther down the almost empty street a woman in bright yellow coveralls pulled a cart from door to door, collecting scrap boxes. Vanja turned away with a shudder and started walking toward the center.

The commune office of Amatka had rounded corners and small, recessed windows. Like all central buildings in all colonies, it was built from concrete, that rare material that the pioneers had brought with them. And like all other things from the old world, concrete didn't need marking to keep its shape. It was solid, comforting. The plaque next to the entrance read *Central building constructed and erected year 15 after arrival. Long live the pioneers! Long live Amatka's commune!*

Immediately inside the entrance, a lanky receptionist sat behind a counter. Vanja showed him her well-thumbed papers and received two copies of a multipage form to fill out. Complete name, age, home colony, temporary address in Amatka, profession, names of children and their place of residence. Education, employment history, and other skills. Was she aware that she might be drafted should any of her skills be needed by the commune during her residence in Amatka? Did she have any diseases or other conditions of which the commune should be informed?

At long last, Vanja handed over the completed forms to the receptionist, who bent over the counter to read them through. He tapped his pen on one of the boxes.

"Here. You haven't filled in the section 'children and their place of residence.'"

"No," said Vanja.

The receptionist tapped his pen on the box where Vanja had given her age. "I see."

Vanja looked down at the floor. Her cheeks were hot.

He asked for her credit book and stamped it with hard little thunks.

"Welcome to Amatka," he said as he handed it back to her. "You're registered as a visitor and may move freely within the colony. Thank you."

"I would also like to fill in a request for information from the archive." Vanja avoided his eyes.

"Next floor, first door on the right." The receptionist turned around and continued stamping documents.

On the next floor, Vanja presented her papers once more and filled in a request for a list of local independent businesses. She was told the procedure would take a few days, thanked the clerk, and left.

The necessary formalities thus taken care of, Vanja visited the clothing depot, Nina's shopping list in hand. After wandering about among work clothes and outer garments at the front of the store, she eventually found her way to the section for sweaters, underclothes, and small items. The store had few visitors at this time of day; the only noise came from a clerk who moved from shelf to shelf with a marking pen, mumbling at each garment.

The fabrics were different here, the materials warm under Vanja's hand. Most clothes were monochrome and bright. Vanja, who was entirely dressed in brown, hesitated. She thought of Nina's blue overalls and Ivar's green shirt and chose clothing in shades of blue and green: a sleeping cap, long underwear, a thick shirt, gloves, socks, a scarf, and an outdoor hat with earflaps and a chin strap. She tried some of the garments on in front of a mirror. She looked a little peculiar with the hat on; her hair stuck out from under the rim and the earflaps stood straight out. She pushed the hat back a little, tucked her hair in, and tied the flaps. That made it look a bit better. She fingered her thin anorak. It was worn at the elbows and shoulders, but it was freshly marked and would do for now. Her trousers were still decent enough, with plenty of space for underclothes now that they had become so loose.

The company hadn't given Vanja extra credit for clothing, but her general disinterest had led to savings substantial enough for all the clothes she'd picked out.

The pharmacy was a couple of doors away. Products were stacked according to category on the shelves, most of them packaged in the red and white of the commune. A couple of dispensers were busy serving customers at the back of the store. Vanja walked slowly along the shelves, reading labels. The range was virtually identical to Essre's, but the proportions were different. Amatka's inhabitants apparently suffered from skin problems: a whole section was devoted to eczema, fungal infections, and other skin conditions. The general-hygiene section was sparse in comparison. Vanja grabbed all boxes not decorated with the commune's colors and filled in a requisition form handed to her by one of the dispensers.

"Do you import any independent products from Essre?" she asked, as the dispenser, a young woman with her hair in a tight bun, packed the items into a brown bag.

The dispenser paused with her hand in the bag. "No. I don't know why we would. We can barely get rid of the stuff made locally. By the independent businesses, I mean. So I don't know how something from Essre would do."

"Why don't people want them, d'you think?"

"You're not from here, are you? It's new. People don't like new. It never turns out well."

The dispenser bagged the last of the items and rummaged for something under the counter. She brought out a couple of pamphlets and stuffed them into the bag.

"Take these, too."

Vanja lugged her heavy load back to the house. She put the bags down on the kitchen table and found some coffee powder in the pantry. It looked homemade, stored in a jar with a mismatched lid. Ivar probably brought coffee mushrooms from work and dried and ground them himself. Vanja filled the pot halfway up with water, added a couple of spoonfuls of powder, and put the pot on the heat. While it simmered, she emptied her bag and went through the bottles, jars, and tubes, arranging them on the table. All in all, she'd brought back thirty-two products from two different manufacturers. When the coffee had finished brewing, it came out of the pot a pale yellow color. Vanja retrieved her notebook out of the satchel and started taking down the names of manufacturers and products, as well as content lists. It was soothing work.

A sudden laugh made her look up. Nina stood by the kitchen door, eyebrows raised. She looked at the jars and bottles covering the table, then at Vanja and then laughed again, not at all in an unfriendly way.

Report 1. Initial Report on Products and Manufacturers

The following is a preliminary report on the occasion of my first visits to stores and the pharmacy, in addition to a few short interviews. I am still awaiting a complete list from the commune office, but have so far identified two independent manufacturers in the hygiene sector. Both specialize in products more expensive and of higher quality than the commune's own. They are not in direct competition with each other, as they have targeted different product areas.

Several persons with whom I have spoken express a dislike for products not the commune's own, but give only vague explanations as to why this is. A common expression is that they simply don't want "new things."

Amatka's First Independent Chemist

Hygiene products of high quality that cost extra credit. The products contain extracts of plants and fungi. The packaging is elegant, in muted colors. According to the pharmacy, this is the most popular alternative product range.

Product Names and Descriptions

Quality Belt. Holder for menstrual liners. 1 per package. A girdle for fastening around the waist, with loops for attaching menstrual pads. The material is somewhat thinner and softer than the commune's own girdles. Girdle and pads are washed normally.

Quality Pad 1. Short menstrual pads, extra thin, 4 per box.

Quality Pad 2. Medium-length menstrual pads, extra thin. 4 per box.

Quality Pad 3. Extra-long menstrual pads, thin and highly absorbent. 2 per box.

Hair Soap 1. Hair soap for greasy hair and dandruff. The ingredients do not differ significantly from the commune's own.

Hair Soap 2. Hair soap for dry hair. Contains extract of cave russula.

Hair Treatment. Softening treatment for hair. Contains extract of slime truffle and soybean oil.

Quality Soap. Liquid soap. Contains extract of cave russula.

Quality Cream. Skin cream. Contains soybean oil and extract of slime truffle.

Cosmetics by Olbris' Lars

Products associated with beauty care. Cost extra credits, except for when prescribed by a physician. The range consists mainly of foundation creams, covering creams, and skin powder. The very wide range of covering creams to hide scars, superficial veins, and cold damage is noteworthy. According to the pharmacy, the products are bought by men and women in equal proportions.

Product Names and Descriptions
Foundation Cream 1. Light foundation cream.

Foundation Cream 2. Medium-colored foundation cream.

Foundation Cream 3. Dark foundation cream.

Covering Cream Red. Covering cream to hide blue areas, such as bruising or dark circles under the eyes.

Covering Cream Yellow. Hides red areas, for example eczema, scars, and acne.

All-cover. Thick covering cream for hiding sores, superficial veins, etc.

Acne Soap. Specialty soap for greasy skin and acne.

Acne Stick. Stick for individual pustules.

Shaving Soap Rich. Shaving soap for dry skin.

Shaving Knife Extra Light. Slender shaving knife that weighs less than the commune's own. Sold with whetstone.

I have attached an assortment of local products along with a copy of the requisition. Also attached is the pharmacy's self-care recommendation pamphlet. As you can see, the instructions differ from Essre's on several points, especially with regards to frequency of washing and cold weather advice.

Best,
Brilars' Vanja Two

Attachment: Hygiene Pamphlet

Publisher: Amatka's communal pharmacy

Washing

Hands, feet, and armpits should be washed with soap and water every morning. Crotch and face should be washed every morning with water only. Hands should also be washed after every toilet visit and before each meal. Baths should be taken once a week. Excess bathing should be avoided, as it may damage the skin's protective layer of natural oils. This is especially important for individuals prone to eczema.

Shaving and Trimming
Men with beards should trim it once a week. Men who shave should do so once a day. Men with dark beard growth may if needed consider one additional shave in the afternoon. The pharmacy discourages all citizens from shaving other body parts.

Intimate Hygiene (for Men)
Genitals should never be washed with soap, but with water only. When washing, gently pull the foreskin back to make sure the area underneath is cleaned. Air-drying is encouraged to lessen the risk of itching.

Intimate Hygiene (for Women)
Genitals should never be washed with soap, but with water only. When menstruating, pads and holders manufactured for this purpose should be used. Pad should be changed every fourth to sixth hour. A used pad is soaked in cold water and then washed in the same way as underclothes.

Dental Hygiene
Teeth should be brushed with brushing powder morning and evening to prevent cavities.

Miscellaneous
Talcum powder may be used to prevent extreme sweating and odor. Rub extra-rich cream onto face and hands in cold weather to avoid eczema and cracked skin.

THIRDAY

Vanja was once again woken by thunder and unable to go back to sleep. She pulled a sweater and trousers over her sleep clothes and went down into the kitchen. According to the schedule on the refrigerator, both Nina and Ivar had morning shifts at work and would need breakfast. Vanja took a pot from the bottom cupboard and checked the pantry. Two bags of porridge flakes sat on the middle shelf: the everyday black bolete and the slightly milder pale polypore. She scooped bolete flakes into the pot and filled it up with two parts water. While the porridge simmered, she made new coffee from yesterday's leftover grounds.

"Hi." Nina had wrapped a large green shawl over her overalls.

She went to the fridge and took out a plate. "Here, we can fry up the leftovers."

They stood side by side in silence, stirring the pot and frying pan. Nina's sleeve brushed gently against Vanja's arm as she poked at the leftovers in the pan.

Ivar came down in time to eat and set the table for three.

"It's not as strong as yours, Ivar," Nina said, sipping the coffee. "I might even avoid a stomachache for once."

"Coffee can never be too strong," Ivar retorted.

"Amatka's coffee consumption is five times higher than the other colonies'," Vanja said.

"How do you know?" Nina asked.

"I proofread a report on coffee consumption once. I tend to . . . pick up facts."

"Ha," said Nina. "Five times, eh? And Ivar makes up half of it."

"I'm self-medicating. I couldn't face the mushroom farm without it." Ivar downed the rest of his coffee and poured himself another cup.

"Ivar doesn't do so well with darkness," Nina said.

Vanja pushed her porridge around with her spoon. "Can't you change jobs? Don't you have rotations?"

Ivar shrugged. "Officially we do. But no one's been allowed to change jobs for years now." He rubbed some yellow gunk from the corner of his eye. "The committee says there aren't enough citizens for rotation to be feasible."

"I'm sure they're doing their best," Nina said.

Ivar rose. "Thanks for breakfast."

Nina poured herself more coffee. Vanja tried to eat some more porridge. It had gone cold and stuck to the roof of her mouth.

"I get so angry with Ivar," Nina said eventually. "I know I shouldn't, but I do. He's down there in the dark, day after day, and gets worse and worse. He could probably get something else to do if he just spoke to the committee. If he just tried a little harder." Nina jabbed her thumb at the door. "It's like he's given up."

Vanja shifted in her seat. "Well, that's none of my business." She scraped the remains of her porridge back into the pot. "I thought I heard thunder this morning," she said. "Outside."

Nina blinked. "What? Oh, that. It's the ice melting."

Vanja slowly set the plate back down on the table. "Ice?"

Nina explained that the lake, which lay just beyond Amatka's eastern border, froze over at night and thawed in the morning. Things had been that way for the last five years. When the sky grew dark, ice formed on the water. After an hour or so, the ice would be thick enough to walk on. The air didn't get colder than usual; whatever it was only affected the water in the lake. And at dawn, the ice broke up again. It was the noise of thawing that Vanja had heard. Nina nodded when Vanja asked if she'd seen it with her own eyes.

"Of course, going there to look was forbidden at first," Nina said. "But when it had been going on unchanged for six months, the committee decided that we should call it a 'normal variation.' So that's what it is now. A normal variation."

"You must have wondered if someone had, well, done something."

"Of course. And maybe someone had. But I don't know anything more about it. And nothing else has happened since."

"Just the lake?"

"Just the lake." Nina got up. "Time to go to my shift."

Vanja had another cup of coffee and washed the breakfast dishes. Then she put on her new undergarments, tied her hat on, and went outside. She walked without an actual goal in mind, slowly ambling in a northeasterly direction, toward the colony's outskirts. The air was damp. Breathing in so much moisture felt unfamiliar. The buildings and people walking between them were all covered in a wet sheen.

Vanja eventually reached the plant houses in the outer ring, their oblong domes translucent, the plants inside a faint green. Planters slowly moved between the rows, watering and weeding. A mumble of voices and song could be heard from inside. Beyond the plant houses, the tundra. Sky and earth blurred together in the distance; for a moment it was as if the colony floated on an island in the void. The thought made Vanja's stomach contract. She turned around and walked back into the colony as quickly as she could without breaking into a run. When she'd made it past the residential ring, she walked into the first public building she saw, oblivious to the words on the facade.

She entered a hallway with coat pegs along the walls. The gray door at the far end was marked DOOR TO THE LIBRARY. Vanja hung her anorak and hat on one of the pegs and opened the door.

The room was small and lined with bookcases, with just enough room for a reading table in the middle. Behind a small counter next to the door sat a plump, bespectacled man with an auburn beard and curly, thinning hair. He was filling in small index cards.

When Vanja closed the door, he put the pen down and looked up with mild brown eyes. "Welcome."

"Thank you." Vanja remained where she was and looked around the room.

"Are you looking for anything in particular?"

"I'm a visitor," Vanja said. "From Essre."

"And you've come here." The librarian brightened visibly. "Are you familiar with Amatka's authors?"

"What? No."

The librarian rose and walked over to a bookcase in the middle of the far wall. He cocked his head and scanned the shelves with his index finger until he located a thin volume. He pulled it out and brushed the cover gently.

"Poetry," he said. "If you want to get to know Amatka, you must read our poetry. This one was written by Berols' Anna. Very concise, very typical of our culture." He offered Vanja the book.

She turned the book over in her hands. *About Plant House 3* had been published twenty years ago: three hundred and sixty-five poems describing Plant House 3 in minute detail. Vanja opened the book to a random page.

at five twenty-two	among the beets
the shift from	blur to acuity
the long furrows	of chalky earth
the sound of water	absorbed by roots

"Is it popular?" Vanja asked.

"Very, very," the librarian replied. "Not as popular as *About Plant House 5*, that's the most popular one by far, but it's on loan at the moment. But you can read them in any order you like. They're written so that the reader can start anywhere."

According to the endpaper, the series consisted of eight books, each one describing a plant house in the outer ring.

"It took Anna ten years to finish the series," he added. "The final book is the most advanced. Extremely dense. Extremely dense," he repeated, nodding for emphasis. "I recommend starting with one of the others."

Vanja held on to the book as she walked along the shelves. The selection was very similar to Essre's. Most of the shelves were filled with nonfiction, histories of the colonies and biographies of the Heroes: citizens who had excelled in their service of the colonies through their actions and sacrifice. Vanja took down *About the Colonies, For Children* from the shelf. They had read from it in class. Vanja had always wanted to go see the other colonies. She had fantasized about sitting on the shores of Balbit or seeing the great factories in Odek.

Colony One, Essre, is the administrative center of all the colonies. Here, the main committee makes decisions that affect all of us. The committee is made up of delegates elected by the people in all the colonies.

Colony Two, Balbit, is a place of science and research; our scientists work tirelessly to find safe and sustainable ways of advancing our quality of life. Balbit sits on the shore of the Southern Ocean. Your teacher will provide any necessary information about the Ocean.

Colony Three, Odek, is the center of industry. Here is manufactured everything a citizen might need: furniture, clothing, tools, and much more.

Colony Four, Amatka, is the agricultural center. Mushrooms of many varieties thrive in the caverns below the colony. Depending on species, they can be used for everything from paper to food.

Colony Five was once the second agricultural center, which exported grains to the other colonies. This colony has suffered cata-

strophic failure and no longer exists. Your teacher will provide any
necessary information.

Vanja turned to the poetry section. It had no equivalent in Essre.
Berols' Anna's poetry cycle was just one of many. Other titles were
About Eight Mushroom Chambers by Idars' Ivar, *About Bodily Varia-*
tions by Torus' Britt, and a thick volume bound in red and marked
only with the words *About Trains.*

She returned to the nonfiction shelves and chose a small volume
entitled *A Short History of Amatka.* After asking for and reviewing
Vanja's papers, the librarian printed a small library card and registered her loan. Then he returned to his index cards and seemed to
instantly forget all about her.

The street outside was almost empty; it was not yet time for the
midday break. Vanja walked homeward.

FOURDAY

Thunder rolled, and Vanja sat upright in her bed. It was morning. The room was freezing; her breath came out in white puffs. Vanja pulled trousers and a shirt on over her sleep clothes. It was too cold to even think about washing.

Amatka felt just as desolate as their parents' collective. Each time Vanja and Ärna went to visit their parents, Ärna seemed comfortable about the whole arrangement; she would move around their parents with ease, accepting the change of environment without complaints. Vanja would miss the dormitory and the noise of other children. Their mother, Britta, was withdrawn and forbidding. She spoke to her children in commands: *eat, sit up straight, go to bed*. She didn't touch them unless she absolutely had to. Lars was different. He would let Vanja hold his hand, even crawl into his lap sometimes, but he let her down again when other adults were around. He shouldn't coddle the children, Britta said. It would make them neurotic.

At night he would always tuck his chidren into bed. This one time, Ärna had fallen asleep straight away. Lars bent down and smoothed the hair from Vanja's forehead. His beard tickled her cheek as his face came even closer. His whispered words smelled of alcohol: *No one knows where we are. But we're not allowed to say that.*

That night, he had remained seated on the edge of her bed, studying Vanja's face for a long moment. *We understand each other, you and I*, he'd said. And then he seemed to sober up and began to tell her a story about how people had found a hole in the world, and passed through, and ended up in this place. But where "this place" was, no one knew, not even the committee.

Downstairs, the kitchen was empty. She found some leftover porridge in the fridge, which she fried and ate in solitude. A formal-looking note on the table informed her that the requested material was now available for collection at the commune office.

The receptionist inspected Vanja's note and papers and went to get a thin brown envelope. Vanja accepted it and exited the central building. The eatery next to the huge arc that was the clinic looked inviting. The interior was simple and tidy, small tables and chairs upholstered in green set along the row of windows. The menu offered coffee and alcohol, pickled mushrooms, a handful of warm dishes. Vanja ordered a pot of coffee and sat down at a table to open her envelope.

The list of manufacturers she'd requested a few days earlier turned out to be very short, with no names other than those she'd already found. She could add information on corporate organization, founding date, and revenue to her notes. All three manufacturers had reported stable revenues for several years. People didn't exactly seem to be clamoring for new products. Vanja sighed to herself.

"It can't be that bad," said a voice behind her.

It was Nina. There were dark circles under her eyes, but she was smiling.

"Hello," she said. "I usually eat here after the night shift." She sat down on the chair opposite and prodded the envelope. "What's that?"

Vanja shrugged. "A list of hygiene-product manufacturers. It's not very exciting."

Nina laughed. The cook rang a little bell over at the counter. Nina got up and returned with a plate piled high with hash and boiled beans. Vanja leafed through the papers while Nina methodically shoveled food into her mouth.

"Why did you get a job like that, really?" Nina said around a mouthful of beans.

Vanja folded and refolded one of the pages. "Ehm . . . I don't know."

"I don't mean to be rude, but it's a pretty odd thing to do. Interview people about how often they wash themselves?"

"Yeah . . . I suppose it's not that great."

Nina gestured with her fork. "I'm not saying it's boring in itself, but you don't exactly seem like you enjoy being around people. I mean this whole thing of making small talk and being friendly. You seem more like Ivar, like you prefer your own company, correct me if I'm wrong. So why pick a job where you have to talk to people? Or was it assigned to you?"

Vanja folded the paper again and again. "I don't know how to answer that."

Nina put her fork down. She rested her forearms on the table and leaned forward. "Let's try this, then," she said. "What's your education?"

"Information assistant." Vanja kept her eyes lowered, but she could feel Nina watching her.

Nina nodded. "That makes sense. And what did you do before you started work at E.H.S.?"

"I wrote pamphlets for the education unit. You know. Those little manuals."

"'How to Stay Healthy' and 'General Clothing Maintenance,' that kind of thing?"

"Yes, exactly. It was sort of fun, actually."

"And how did you end up at E.H.S.?"

"It was Ärna. My sister. She knew the founder of the company. She thought I needed to get out and meet people." Vanja unfolded the paper and folded it in the other direction. "So I got an interview."

Nina pushed the empty plate into Vanja's field of vision. "And how's that working out for you?"

"Eh. It's okay. Or . . . I guess that's irrelevant."

"Okay, you're going to have to relax a bit, Vanja. I know you've come to do a job, but you're welcome here. I really enjoy having you."

Vanja looked up. Nina was leaning in even closer, head tilted to one side. She smiled when Vanja met her gaze. The green in her irises was speckled with brown. Fine lines radiated from the corners of her eyes. They deepened as Nina smiled again.

"There you are," Nina said. "Hi."

"Hi."

"I mean it. I'm glad you've come."

Vanja felt her face flush and looked down at the table again. "I'm glad to be here," she mumbled.

"Except that you hate your job," Nina added.

"Except that. I don't think I'm very good at this. I mean . . . there aren't any instructions for what I should be doing. I've tried to do some research, but . . . I don't even know what they want." Vanja fingered the coffeepot. "What if I do it wrong? What if I'm here for three weeks and come back with information they can't use?"

Nina laughed. "It's not you—it's your job that's completely absurd. Well, all right. I'll help you out, if you'll let me." She poked at the crumpled paper in Vanja's hand. "You've got your statistics there. We'll get you some workplace visits. We can start at the clinic, and then you can do a field study with Ivar. And then we'll persuade Ulla to talk a little about what it was like back when she was young, so you get the historical aspect. And then you'll have a nice little report for your boss."

Vanja considered this. "It sounds good, actually."

"Then that's decided!" Nina got up. "I'm going home to get some sleep. I'm on the day shift tomorrow. You can come with me to the clinic then."

Vanja stayed for a while after Nina had left. Nina's familiarity was both unsettling and liberating. It was impossible to lie to her. If Vanja wasn't careful, Nina would soon realize what a failure she was dealing with, and then she'd back right off. It was almost comforting to know that beforehand.

She tore a page off her notepad and wrote a short letter.

Dear Ärna,

Have been in Amatka for a few days. It is cold but my hosts are friendly. Am doing research. Do not know how long it will take, but have a ticket for a trip back in three weeks' time, so should be finished by then. I hope Per is fine and that Pia and Dorit are well behaved in the children's house.

Vanja folded the paper and packed her things into the satchel. When she exited the eatery, she turned toward the center again, heading for a little all-purpose store, where she bought a couple of necklaces made of spotted pebbles from the lake. She moved on to the post office and sent the letter and the gifts to Ärna.

Back in her room, Vanja wrapped herself in the pink duvet and put the two library books down next to her on the bed. *A Short History of Amatka* described the pioneers and their hard work to build the colony—twice. According to the book, Amatka had first been built as a coastal colony in the style of Balbit. Shortly after construction commenced, the lake's water level suddenly rose, forcing the colony to move. Most of the building materials could be transported inland, but some had been lost.

A section of the book was dedicated to the Heroes, pioneers who had contributed to the colonies with exceptionally hard work and initiative. Benins' Yara and her group, who built the railroad from Essre to Amatka sleeper by sleeper. Haras' Samir, the brilliant scientist who prevented an epidemic by synthesizing a cure from mushrooms. Danlas' Åke, who organized the first children's house. And

Speaker Hedda, the greatest Hero of them all. When the old world was decadent and doomed to ruin, Speaker Hedda found a way into a new world and led her people there. No one had ever explained exactly where the old world was, or what it was like. It was irrelevant. They were here now, in the new world, where they had built the ideal society.

Another section of the book featured Amatka's literature, especially its poetry. Berols' Anna had a whole page to herself. In the picture she was solemn, of early middle age, with severe dark eyebrows over a soft face. According to the caption, Berols' Anna was one of the people who died in the fire in Leisure Center Three. Vanja leafed through the book until she found a chapter with that title.

On Thirday of the twelfth month, in year 90 A.A., a fire broke out in Leisure Center Three, where almost a hundred citizens had gathered to take part in Amatka's annual poetry and music festival. The fire started in the coatroom, where an electrical component short-circuited and ignited the clothes on the walls, generating massive amounts of smoke. The fire quickly spread to the rest of the hall. The final death count was 103, with most victims succumbing to smoke inhalation. We mourn our comrades and honor their memory by looking forward, thankful for their many contributions to the commune.

"Looking forward" meant that this was no longer an accepted topic of conversation. Perhaps the accident was someone's fault: a decision made somewhere that would have made the committee look bad. Or people had mourned too much and for too long. That wasn't proper, either. One should be grateful and look forward.

Vanja put the book down and opened *About Plant House 3*. The text was difficult to read at first. Every sentence had been whittled down until only the absolutely necessary words remained. Every one of those words was precise; it could have been lifted out of the text and hold enough meaning in itself. In Berols' Anna's poetry, all things became completely and self-evidently solid. The world gained consistency in the life cycle of plants, the sound of a rake in the soil. Breathing became easier. Vanja read the book from cover to cover. When she had followed Plant House 3 through an entire year, from harvest to harvest, the room had darkened. Downstairs, someone clattered with pots and pans.

"Would you help Ulla with the marking?" Nina called over her shoulder as Vanja came downstairs. "We're to do it a couple of times a week."

"Sure," Vanja said.

Ulla opened the door almost as soon as Vanja knocked.

"Nina told me to help you mark things," Vanja said.

"Ah," Ulla said. "I can't manage that on my own, can I. How kind of you."

She showed Vanja into a little hallway, where the doors to all three rooms stood open. Two rooms were completely empty. The third, the room directly below Vanja's, was furnished. Ulla had a table with two chairs, a bed, and a cabinet; books cluttered every surface.

"How are you finding Amatka, then?" Ulla said.

"It's fine," Vanja replied.

"I heard you had an accident."

Vanja nodded. "I did."

Ulla tutted. "That won't do."

"I know," Vanja said. "I'm sorry."

"Oh, don't apologize. Once is just an accident, after all." Ulla winked at her.

Vanja went through the other rooms to mark the lights, windowsills, and doors, then returned to Ulla's room. Ulla was already busy marking her things, one by one. It became clear why she needed help: she owned more things than anyone Vanja had ever seen. She turned to the left wall and a rickety shelf.

Wedged between a copy of *About Bodily Variations* and *A Biogra-*

phy of Speaker Hedda was a slim volume with the word *Anna* hand-written on the spine. No *About*, just *Anna*, as if the book was named Anna. One couldn't name a book anything other than BOOK, or start the title with anything other than "About . . ." Naming an object something else, even accidentally, was forbidden.

Vanja drew the book out and opened it. Poetry, on what looked like good paper, handwritten in faded blue ink:

> *we speak*   *of new worlds*
> *we speak*   *of new lives*
> *we speak*   *to give ourselves*
> *to become*

Ulla gently took the book out of Vanja's hands. "That's personal, dear," she said.

"Is that Berols' Anna?"

Ulla nodded. "Yes, it is."

"But it's handwritten," Vanja said.

"It was a gift." Ulla tucked the book back in between the other volumes.

"What does she mean, to become?"

Ulla looked Vanja up and down, as if she was examining her. "I might tell you sometime," she said eventually.

"I read about the fire," Vanja said.

Ulla's mouth twisted. "Right. The fire."

"What's that?"

"Nothing. We're looking forward, after all." Ulla turned away. "Go on with the marking, dear."

FIFDAY

It wasn't yet light out. Nina and Vanja had a slow morning meal of fried porridge. The coffee Nina had made was acrid and bright yellow.

"I've arranged so you can go with me all morning," said Nina. "After that I'll have to take care of patients."

The streets were nearly deserted. Amber light pooled under the streetlights. The white arc of the clinic building made everything else look very small.

Nina brought Vanja in through a side entrance. They entered a low hall almost entirely taken up by two gray vehicles with the words TRANSPORT VEHICLE stenciled on their sides. Nina led her through the garage and a pair of double doors. On the other side was a long corridor with doors spaced evenly along its white walls. A murmur of low voices and shuffling feet, punctuated by mechanical beeps. The air smelled of disinfectant. Vanja had forgotten how heavy that smell was, how it made her ribs feel too tight.

"Are you okay?" Nina asked beside her.

Vanja nodded automatically.

Nina continued down the corridor. "Anyway, this is the emergency room," she said over her shoulder.

"It's very calm," Vanja said.

"There's rarely any action in there."

Nina made an abrupt left turn and opened a door to a stairwell. They climbed two stairs and emerged into a new corridor. The atmosphere was livelier here: staff in white overalls, patients in wheelchairs and on stretchers. Nina brought Vanja to a desk where she was asked to sign in. She accepted the small tag that said CARD FOR VISITORS, and followed Nina to a room lined with cabinets and shelves stacked with work clothes. Nina retrieved two pairs of white overalls and handed Vanja one of them, along with a pair of shoe covers. She opened one of the cabinets and took out a pair of white indoor shoes.

"You can put your clothes in here."

Vanja's overalls were too large. Nina pulled on hers and smiled as Vanja rolled her sleeves and legs up.

"It doesn't matter which size you pick—they never quite fit." Nina pointed to her own overalls, which were too short in the sleeves but too long in the legs. "The important thing is that they're not tight across your bottom. That could make lifting patients embarrassing." She winked.

Vanja took her notepad and a pencil from her satchel and hung it in the cabinet. "I'm ready."

The smell of disinfectant washed over them as they returned to the corridor, and Vanja's stomach turned.

"Are you really okay?" Nina asked again. She leaned closer. "You're pale."

"Eh. It's just the smell." Vanja laid an arm across her belly.

"Just let me know if you need to go outside."

Vanja straightened. "No, no need. Can we get started?"

Nina looked at her for a moment, frowning. Then she nodded and continued down the corridor.

They spent the morning visiting the different units. Amatka's population suffered from lifestyle diseases and work injuries: bad backs from work in the plant houses and the mushroom farm; cardiovascular disease; osteoporosis. And depression, everywhere depression.

"It's a little darker here than in Essre, have you noticed?" Nina said.

Vanja shook her head. "I think dawn and dusk come at roughly the same times as usual."

"No, it's not that. The daylight is weaker. It's at ninety percent of the brightness in Essre."

"Who says?"

"The research department."

"Oh." Vanja considered this. "What does it feel like?"

"Feels? I'm used to it. But you must have noticed it's dimmer."

"Maybe a little . . . No. Not really."

"Well. That's how it is, in any case. That's why we have the light rooms." Nina pushed open a pair of double doors.

The corridor they entered was more brightly lit. The doors on either side had little windows that revealed rooms entirely furnished in white. Every room was populated by people in white coats who sat in white reclining chairs, their legs wrapped in white blankets. Ceiling lamps spread a bluish-white light.

"Anyone can go in here when they need to," Nina said, and nodded at the door closest to them. "Some come every day. Most people come about once a week or every other week."

"Does it help?" Vanja squinted at the patients. Most were reading books or deep in conversation.

"It does. Most of the time. And don't forget we have coffee, too." Nina winked at Vanja. "But I suppose we're all a little melancholy, even those of us who aren't ill."

Nina left Vanja in the clinic's storeroom and went to take care of some administrative task or other. Vanja busied herself making an inventory of the hygiene products stacked on the shelves: soap, rubbing alcohol, cream, lubricant, disinfectant. The unease that the stench permeating the corridors had stirred up in her chest slowly dissipated. It crept back when the door opened and Nina came back in.

"How are you doing?"

Vanja frowned at her list. "Not sure any of this is useful. You only use the commune's products. Are there things you don't stock? Things you might need?"

Nina sucked her front teeth. "Don't think so."

Vanja put a bottle of lotion back on the shelf. "I'm done. Let's move on."

"There are only a few more units left to see. This way."

They went down a set of stairs and into yet another white corridor, where a pair of double doors were marked DOORS TO FERTILITY UNIT. Nina pushed the doors open, releasing a fresh puff of disinfectant smell. The stink crept into Vanja's nostrils and down into her stomach, sending it into a new spasm. Nina paused with a hand on the right door and looked over her shoulder.

"What's wrong?"

Vanja shook her head. "We don't need to go in there," she said.

"Why not?"

"How about we just say we're done."

Nina gazed at Vanja and then at the sign on the door. "All right."

She turned back and headed in the opposite direction. Vanja followed her. They were alone in the corridor; the sound of Nina's shoes echoed against the walls.

"Do you have children, Vanja?" Nina's voice was low.

"No." The word sounded harsh.

Nina's voice softened further. "You've been to that kind of unit quite recently, haven't you?"

Vanja glanced sideways. Nina's face didn't have the expression of sickly pity that her sister's and Marja's had had. On the contrary, she looked a little weary. Vanja nodded and squeezed her lips shut so they wouldn't quiver. Her eyes stung.

Nina sighed and ran the back of her hand down Vanja's arm. "It's hard."

"Yes." Vanja pulled away.

"I'm sure they did everything they could for you. Sometimes that's just how it is. It happens more often than people think."

Vanja hummed and crossed her arms over her chest.

"I should warn you, our children are visiting this weekend," Nina said as they reached the end of the corridor. "If that's too difficult, then . . . we could find some other solution."

"No. It's not that."

"Then what is it?"

"Uh." Vanja's face was warm and tingly. The words wouldn't quite get into sequence. She breathed in and out a few times. "It's not that. I don't care about your children. It's . . . I don't care about them."

Nina stood still, studying her with a deep frown.

"I'll be going now. Thank you," said Vanja. "I can find my way to the dressing room."

Nina nodded slowly. The frown didn't disappear. "You're welcome."

Vanja walked back the way they had come, fighting the impulse to run. As she walked past a set of double doors, they opened to let through an orderly pushing a wheelchair. The woman in the wheelchair was dressed in a paper gown. Her temples were shaved and scabbed over. She stared blindly into the air. The orderly gave Vanja a sharp glance and moved past her.

The woman had been taken care of, like Lars had been taken care of, like everyone who spoke out of turn were taken care of. There was no death penalty in the colonies. Dissidents had to be stopped from endangering the community, however. The procedure that destroyed the brain's speech center was an elegant solution. Vanja ran the last few steps to the exit.

The cold air in the street rinsed the clinic's stench out of Vanja's nostrils. Few people were out at this time of day, but she still felt claustrophobic. The whole colony and its buildings crowded her. She went home to pack her satchel.

Vanja followed the fat water conduit eastward. To her right and left the plant houses marked Amatka's perimeter. Beyond the plant houses there was only the tundra and a narrow path along the irrigation pipeline. The lake was visible as a broad gray band on the horizon. It separated ground and sky, made them two distinct units.

It was a longer walk down to the bay than Nina had said. A slight breeze blew across the tundra, and Amatka's sounds gradually faded behind her. The silence made her ears ring.

She had been outside a colony once before, beyond the protective shell of civilization or a vehicle. Leaving the colony wasn't forbidden as such, but straying outside the narrow safe zone was intensely discouraged. Good citizens kept inside the plant-house ring. Only eccentrics ventured farther out willingly.

East of Essre, out on the steppe, there was a place about which everyone knew, but of which it was inappropriate to speak. Lars had spoken about it sometimes, only to Vanja and in whispers, when Vanja and Ärna came for their weekend visits.

When the pioneers arrived, Lars said, they discovered they weren't the first. Out on the steppe, east of what would become Essre, they came across a cluster of empty buildings. Whoever had once lived there had left no other trace. The architecture was alien, the proportions inhuman: huge, lumbering houses with odd angles. And despite the fact that the buildings lacked anything resembling markings or letters, they were completely solid. The place was off-limits, but everyone knew that this was where they put criminals: far away from everyone else, in a place they couldn't ruin. *One wonders who the builders were,* Lars would breathe, *and why we can't go there. Nobody knows where we are. But we're not allowed to speak of it.*

Then Vanja came home on a weekend visit, and Britta told her that Lars had been taken away. He was disloyal and had to be contained. Vanja knew where they had taken him. She snuck out of the house and ran out onto the steppe. She walked for what felt like hours before Essre's lights finally faded behind her. The sky had begun to brighten into gray when she reached the top of a low hill. Ahead of her, the ground sloped down into a flat valley. And there they were, the strange buildings. She approached not completely knowing what she would find.

Now beneath Amatka's silence, there was the gentle surging of waves lapping against the rocky shore. A gentle breeze brought with it the scent of something wet and somehow bright; it must be what lakes smell like. A little ways to the south along the beach rose an angular and broken silhouette: the first Amatka, the one that was never finished.

Vanja found a large, flat rock by the water's edge. She dropped her satchel on the ground and took out two blankets; she spread one of them over the rock, then wrapped herself in the other and sat down to watch the fading of the light.

The process was so quick she could see it happen. A whiteness appeared at the water's edge, and spread like a web across the lake with a crackling noise. The water underneath was dark at first, then grew cloudy as if fogging over. After an hour or so, the ice had cleared into a pure, bottomless black.

Vanja left her blankets and satchel behind and tested the ice with her foot. The surface was uneven and firm. Getting traction was easy; the ice received Vanja's footsteps with a blunt, scraping sound. The sky above her had darkened, but the glow it reflected from Amatka's lights reached all the way to the lake. Vanja took a few more steps out onto the ice and looked back over her shoulder. Far away, the plant-house bubbles shone in yellow and white. She turned toward the lake again, Amatka's light warm against her back. No civilization this way, no human life; just the ice and the tundra and the devouring darkness. For a moment, she thought she saw a flickering reflection from across the lake, so faint it might as well have been one of those flashes the eye creates in darkness.

Vanja rubbed her eyes with her mittens and returned to the beach. The darkness pulled at her back. She packed her blankets into the satchel as quickly as she could and walked, almost ran, toward the warm glow of the plant houses.

SIXDAY

The next morning, not quite as early, it was Ivar who knocked on Vanja's door. The coffee he'd made was even stronger than yesterday's. Nina had already left for work. "Have you been to the mushroom chambers before?" Ivar asked as they sat down for breakfast.

"Never."

"You'll see," Ivar said. "I think you might find it interesting."

The entrance to the mushroom chambers lay to the southwest, in the middle of the third quadrant. The low building aboveground housed a canteen, changing rooms, and offices. Ivar showed Vanja into a room lined with shelves. He picked out overalls, rubber boots, gloves, and hats for both of them.

When they'd changed into their protective clothing, and Ivar had made sure Vanja's pants and sleeves were properly tucked into her boots and gloves, he opened a door at the other end of the room. A wide, dimly lit set of stairs zigzagged downward.

At the bottom, they stopped in front of a heavy door, which Ivar pulled open. Sconces spread a mild light across the white walls of the corridor beyond. The sharp smell of detergent stung Vanja's nostrils. When Ivar pushed open the door at the other end of the corridor, a damp chill rushed over them from the gloom beyond the threshold.

The gradual dimming of the light had made it easier to adapt to the semidarkness. The vaulted tunnel stretched as far as Vanja could see; broad shelves ran along both sides of it. Every surface was covered in a layer of soil. Out of the soil sprung white, round mushrooms. "It's not as dark as this everywhere," Ivar said behind her. "This is just the section for photosensitive mushrooms."

Vanja nodded. "I understand," she added when she realized Ivar might not have been able to see the gesture.

Under the layers of damp, soil, and detergent there was a whiff of something sickly that stuck at the back of Vanja's throat. "Ugh," she said. "The smell."

Ivar came up next to her and prodded at the shelf closest to them. "It's the fertilizer. The mushrooms are grown in composted feces."

They moved on along the shelves. Eventually the light grew stronger, and they entered a hall where the mushrooms on the shelves were taller and plumper, with broad caps. Disk-shaped growths covered the walls. A couple of technicians on narrow ladders were busy carefully prying the lumps off a wall. "Polypores?" Vanja asked.

Ivar nodded. "Exactly. Those are pale polypores—they're ground down for porridge and custard. It's the same kind of porridge we had this morning."

"Can you use them for other things, too?"

"Not really. They're very tough and stringy, so it's the only way you can make them edible."

They came to a fork in the tunnel. New fungi appeared on the shelves: brown agarics with low, wide caps; yellow tangled clavaria that grew in tall clusters; and small, black funnel chanterelles. There were also mushrooms she didn't recognize: thick-stalked mushrooms with tiny caps, mushrooms sheathed in slimy membranes, mushrooms spread flat across a wall. Ivar named each one and described their uses. Enormous polypores covered one of the tunnels from floor to ceiling, the smallest ones the size of dinner plates. Mycopaper base, Ivar explained. "There are other sections," he said, "for medicinal use. We don't allow visitors in there, though. Some of the fungi are poisonous."

"How big is this structure?" Vanja asked.

"About as big as Amatka."

The next door opened into a large, brightly lit chamber taken up almost completely by the four shiny cylinders in the middle of the room. Ivar pointed. "This is where we grow the mycoprotein."

He guided Vanja up a small ladder leaning against the side of the cylinder closest to them and opened a small hatch. Through a thick window, Vanja could see a brown mass that covered the inside of the cylinder. "It doesn't look very tasty right now, does it?" Ivar said. "It gets better once it's processed."

They left the chamber through a door on the other side of the chamber and emerged in the part of the tunnel they'd first set out from. Vanja paused to let her eyes readjust to the sudden darkness. The white mushroom clusters slowly reappeared in front of her.

When they came back up to the surface, they went back into the changing room, and Ivar took Vanja's protective clothing and put it down a hatch together with his own. They washed all parts of themselves that hadn't been protected by an unbroken stretch of fabric: wrists, ankles, heads, hair.

The canteen served a stew of root vegetables and mycoprotein, ladled into large bowls. The farmers ate like they worked, in slow silence. Vanja and Ivar sat down by one of the long tables. Vanja found herself lowering her voice to a near-whisper.

"What is your situation with hygiene products?"

"Right. That's the reason why I really wanted you to visit." Ivar jerked his head toward the other guests in the canteen. "Look at their hands and necks."

More than half of the farmers had sizable red blotches on their necks and around their wrists. In some cases the rash had developed into full-blown eczema, scaly and wet-looking. "It's the laundry detergent and the soap," Ivar said. "We have to kill off any spores and microorganisms so they don't spread outside the farms. Some of the species are very aggressive. But the fungicides are so strong. People get rashes."

"What happens if the spores get out?" Vanja asked.

"There are some species that tend to invade buildings," Ivar replied. "It's a sort of dry rot. Breaks down structural integrity."

"You haven't complained about the fungicides to the committee?" Vanja reminded herself to spoon some of the stew into her mouth.

"Of course we have. But nothing's happening." Ivar scowled.

Vanja nodded. "I'll report back to the company."

She glanced at Ivar. He'd been calm, almost cheerful, in the mushroom chambers. Back in the canteen, his frown was now back.

"Why did you start working in the chambers, Ivar?"

Ivar shrugged a little. "I like growing things." He filled his spoon. "And the quiet."

"But it's dark."

"I've tried to transfer to the plant houses. But the committee won't let me."

Vanja's spoon clattered against the bowl. "The committee, again."

"Don't know if there's any point trying again. I'm in line already. It'll happen when it happens, I guess." Ivar put his spoon down and got to his feet. "I have to go back downstairs. You know the way out, right?"

Vanja nodded. She stayed for a while after Ivar had left. The mushroom farmers moved like they were still in the chambers, slowly and methodically. A low murmur of scattered conversation billowed along the floor. When Vanja returned to the street, the outside noises grated on her ears.

Vanja came home to find Nina and Ulla at the kitchen table. Two girls in red children's house overalls were seated across from them. They turned their heads in unison to look at Vanja as she entered. Both of them had inherited Nina's loose curls, the older girl in Ivar's rich shade of brownish black, the younger in the metallic red Nina must have had as a child. They watched Vanja intently.

"This is Tora and Ida," Nina said. "And this is Vanja, the one I told you about. Say hello to Vanja now, girls. Up you get."

The girls immediately stood up. They each stuck out their right hand. "Ninivs' Tora Four," said the eldest. "Ninivs' Ida Four," said the youngest, lisping through the gap of a missing front tooth.

"Brilars' Vanja Essre Two." Vanja shook hands with each of them.

Tora and Ida studied her with solemn eyes and then returned to the table.

"Tora and Ida just told me what they've learned this week." Nina fetched a cup from the kitchen cabinet and poured Vanja coffee.

Vanja sat down at the head of the table and sipped from her cup. The girls' eyes were fixed on her, brown and green.

Nina smiled at them. "What else have you learned?"

"We've memorized mushrooms," Tora offered. "And the shape of the world," Ida added.

"They learn everything by rote these days." Nina took a sip of her own coffee. "Apparently they're not supposed to have books anymore. The teachers claim the children learn quicker without them."

"Quit using books?" Vanja frowned.

"Go upstairs to Ulla's room and do some marking," Nina told the children. "If that's all right, Ulla?"

Ulla shrugged. "If it gives them something to do."

Tora and Ida left the table without a word.

"Something's going on with the good paper," Nina said. "It's the same thing over at the clinic. We get less and less good paper, so we have to start committing things like schedules and routines to memory. We've even had to start using mycopaper for the medical records."

"But that won't work."

"No. We've had to bring more people in just to retype the records before the old ones reach their scrap-by date."

Vanja glanced at Nina. "But why? Do you think we're running out?"

"They say the good paper is needed elsewhere."

"And you haven't thought to ask why?" Ulla said.

Nina waved her hand dismissively. "I'm sure they'll tell us if it's important. Until then, we probably shouldn't talk about it."

"But it's good paper, it's okay. It's not mycopaper," Vanja said. "We can talk about good paper as much as we like."

"But still," Nina said.

"We all know something will happen sooner or later," Ulla said. "We're running out of good paper."

"I'm not stupid," Nina cut off. "I just don't see why you feel a need to talk about it."

The sound of the girls' high-pitched voices could be heard through the ceiling: *Bed! Chair! Cabinet! Lamp!* Nina put her arm around Vanja's shoulders. Vanja was suddenly very aware of her scent: sweet, spicy, with an underlying hint of something she couldn't name. The heat from Nina's arm radiated through the fabric of her shirt.

"Hear how good they're doing? We'll be fine," Nina said. "Now stop dwelling on it."

Ivar and Nina were both very physical with the children. Tora and Ida always had a parent's hand resting on their shoulder, or arm around their waist, or fingers running through their hair. The girls responded by jumping down from the lap they'd been lifted onto, sliding out from underneath the hand, ducking away from the fingers. They clung to each other instead. Their body language was completely synchronized. At bedtime, they said good night and ran up the stairs before their parents could reply.

"Every time they visit, it's like they've forgotten who we are," Nina said when the sound of footsteps had faded. "But they do become more friendly with time."

According to the committee, it wasn't healthy for parents and children to be too close. They were to socialize once a week, to satisfy the emotional needs that unfortunately still plagued many and that, if entirely neglected, could needlessly cause neuroses. But a bond that grew too strong made the children dependent and less inclined to feel solidarity with the commune.

At the children's house, Vanja had always longed for the weekend, when Lars would stand in the doorway to the dormitory, and she would walk—but not too quickly—over to him and take his callused hand, and he would look down at her with brimming eyes and say: *There you are.* Once, he knelt down and hugged her. Then Teacher Elin had taken him out into the corridor and talked to him for a long time. After that, he just held out his hand.

SEVENDAY

Sevendays were for wholesome fun with family and friends, and most citizens had the day off. Parents could spend time with their offspring, if they wanted to. Everyone would visit one of the leisure centers to play games, sing together, and enjoy a delicious Sevenday dinner.

Vanja declined to join Nina and Ivar, telling them that she'd come by later. She wouldn't have to be there until evening anyway. She slid her book into her anorak pocket, so she would have something to hide behind once she got to the center, and walked out of the house with no particular goal in mind.

The library's window was lit and the door unlocked. Inside, the librarian sat at his desk with a thermos and a pile of books. "It's Sevenday," he said without looking up.

"I'm sorry," Vanja said. "I'll leave."

She paused. The librarian's posture seemed off somehow: slumped and tense at the same time. When she didn't leave, he looked up. His eyes were bloodshot and swollen, and salty white lines ran down his cheeks. He cleared his throat and tried to smile. His voice was rough when he spoke. "You borrowed *About Plant House 3*, didn't you. Did you like it?"

Vanja nodded.

The librarian rubbed his eyes, sniffled, and rose. "I suppose we'd better get you another one, since you're here."

Vanja followed him to the poetry section. The librarian ran his finger along the shelf. Between the books were gaps that Vanja hadn't seen before. She peered around the room. In some of the bookcases, whole sections gaped empty. The librarian handed Vanja a small volume. The cover was stamped ABOUT PLANT HOUSE 7.

"Thank you," Vanja said. "Have people been borrowing a lot recently?" she added, and waved her book at the shelves around them.

The librarian cleared his throat again. "No." He walked over to his desk and picked up the topmost book, which he leafed through without really looking. "I'm culling." He put the book back down, took his glasses off, and pressed his palms against his eyes.

Vanja stood very still by the poetry bookcase. It wasn't proper to barge into other people's private affairs. But the fact that he was alone in the library on a Sevenday, with tears running down his face . . . The librarian let out a long breath and sniffled.

"Are you all right?" Vanja finally asked.

The librarian drew a shaky breath. "I'm culling." It came out as a whimper.

He breathed in and out a few times, then rummaged through one of his pockets, pulled out a wrinkled handkerchief, and wiped his face and beard. Then he blew his nose and put his glasses back on. "I'm culling." This time, his voice was steady; only the tears in his eyes betrayed him. "The committee has ordered me to remove half of the books here," he continued. "Anything not . . . essential . . . is to be destroyed and recycled. Because the committee needs good paper."

Vanja frowned. "What for?"

"I don't know!" The librarian waved his arm at the bookcases. "These books are going to disappear forever so the committee can have . . . forms or special paper to wipe their fat arses with." He drew a shaky breath. "And I have to decide which ones to destroy. And they won't be replaced, do you understand? They'll never come back. Ever." New tears trickled down his cheeks. "Everything that's just . . .

useless entertainment. Everything that only exists to make you feel good. It has to go."

"That's horrible," Vanja said. Speaking the words aloud sent little shocks through her body.

The librarian stopped himself and slapped his forehead. "But what am I saying? I didn't mean anything by it. You understand that, don't you? That I didn't mean anything by it. Of course the committee's decision is for the good of the commune. You know that, right? I was just upset. Could we leave it at that? I didn't mean what I said. Okay?"

"But I agreed with you."

They looked at each other in silence. "So you did," the librarian said slowly.

Vanja's back was itching, as though someone was standing behind her. She looked over her shoulder. Nobody there, of course. But someone could be, at any moment. "I have to go," she said, and held out her hand. "Brilars' Vanja Essre Two."

The librarian took her hand and shook it firmly. "Samins' Evgen."

"We talked about books today."

Evgen gave her a sudden smile. "If you want to talk about books again, I'll be here."

Back in the street, Vanja shoved her hands into her pockets. *About Plant House 7* was in the left one. She'd forgotten to register the loan. It would have to wait. A strange energy was running through her. What if someone had overheard them? She reminded herself to breathe.

The double doors of Leisure Center Two were wide open. Music and voices spilled out into the street. Inside, citizens were divided into groups, engaged in fun activites. It was a packed full-day program: sack racing, three-legged racing, ring tossing, ball games, dancing. The sound of an old dancing tune could be heard now: *The farmer stands like so, watch her walk and watch her sow.*

Soon, it would be time for the communal evening meal. Children without active parents would be seated among the other households. Everyone would stand up and sing "The Pioneer Song." Then they would sit down to eat. The children would tell everyone what they'd learned at the children's house during the week. Their elders would listen and praise them for their diligence.

Vanja stepped inside and gave the clerk by the entrance her name and designation. She continued into the main hall without bothering to hang her anorak up in the coatroom. The hall was long and narrow; high above, square windows close to the ceiling let in the last gray light of evening. Below each window hung posters adorned with quotes and words of wisdom from the Heroes. The long tables in the back of the hall were already set with plates and utensils. Cooking smells spread all the way from the kitchen doors by the stage at the other end of the room. In the space between the stage and the tables, children danced in a ring. Their parents stood around them, clapping a rhythm on their thighs. Vanja found a seat as far back among the tables as possible. She glimpsed Nina and Ivar, playing awkwardly with their daughters in the crowd. She sat still and let the cacophony wash over her until it was late enough to make absconding acceptable.

At home, it was as Vanja fumbled for the light switch that her foot landed in something with a wet noise. The sound traveled up her leg as a cold shock. She forced herself to lift her foot very slowly and then turned the light on.

It was the suitcase. It had been out of sight under the bed, and she hadn't marked it for several days. It had been so worn, the text on the lid almost erased. She should have scrapped it. Now it was too late. The whitish gloop it had dissolved into had spread across nearly half the floor. It stuck to the sole of her boot. Nothing but her boot between her and that substance. She didn't know what would happen if she touched it, but it would spread to other objects if she didn't act fast. Vanja struggled to untie her laces and kicked the boot away. She rushed down the stairs and collided with Nina in the coatroom.

She grabbed Nina's shoulders to stay upright, sending her stumbling backward into the front door.

"What? What is it?" Nina shouted.

"Don't go upstairs, don't go upstairs." Vanja's heart beat out syncopes against her rib cage. "There's gloop on the floor."

Nina exhaled slowly through her nose. "You stay here. I'll get a cleaner."

Vanja sat down on the stairs. Ivar came in; he was alone. He glanced at her and then up the stairs. Vanja shook her head, and Ivar pressed his lips together. He went into the kitchen.

Nina came back with two cleaners in yellow overalls in tow. They carried shovels and boxes. She ushered Vanja into the kitchen so the cleaners could pass.

Nina motioned for Vanja to sit down next to Ivar. She poured her a cup of cold coffee.

"Are the girls at the children's house?" Vanja said, just to fill the silence.

"We have to make sure we mark things here," Nina said.

Vanja looked into her cup. "It was an old suitcase."

Nina snorted. "Then you should have had the sense to scrap it."

"I'm sorry. I didn't think it would happen so quickly."

"Maybe it's different in Essre," Ivar said. "Maybe you can afford to be a little careless there. Because there are more of you, I mean. More people who can mark things."

"That doesn't work here," Nina filled in.

"I get it," Vanja said. "Please, forgive me." She pulled her unshod foot into her lap and warmed it between her hands.

They sat in silence, nursing their cups. The cleaners walked up and down the stairs several times. Creaking and scraping noises could be heard from the second floor. Eventually one of the cleaners came into the kitchen. Her face was sweaty.

"We're done," she said. "It had barely spread at all."

"Spread?" Vanja exclaimed.

The others looked at her. "She's from Essre," Nina said after a brief pause.

"Aha. Hey," the cleaner said. "MOSO, remember?"

"Mark often, scrap often," Vanja replied automatically.

"Here, that means often. Or it'll spread. You'll keep an eye on her, yeah?" The cleaner gave them a wave and left.

"Well, then." Ivar pushed his chair back. "Let's see what's what, then."

The corner where the bed had stood was empty. The cleaners' tools had left long scratches in the floor. Vanja's boot was nowhere to be seen. "This is 'barely'?" Vanja said. She took a step into the room. The foot without a boot tingled.

Ivar let out a short laugh. "It's always 'barely.'"

Vanja looked around the room. It would be very uncomfortable to sleep on the floor. And so close to where it had happened.

"You can sleep in my room," Nina offered. "We'll get you a new bed tomorrow."

Vanja hadn't been into Nina's room before; the door had always been closed. It was more austere and unadorned than she had thought it would be. The bed was immaculately made, the cabinets shut. There was no desk. A poster of an old evening poem sat on the wall:

> *as evening comes*
> *we keep in mind*
> *when morning's here*
> *all will remain;*
> *as morning comes*
> *we keep in mind*
> *today's the same*
> *as yesterday.*

Nina stripped down to her green underpants and a shirt that fit snuggly across her shoulders and upper arms. They were beautiful shoulders, wide and rounded. She wasn't wearing a bra; her breasts moved freely under her shirt. Vanja turned away and peeled off her outmost layer of clothes, folding and stacking them carefully. She was afraid to turn around.

"We'll have to lie on our sides," Nina said. "No room for sleeping on your back." She was already in bed, facing the wall.

Vanja slipped in under the duvet next to Nina and stared out into the room. "Are you angry?" she asked.

"I got over it hours ago," Nina mumbled. "But if you steal the duvet or snore. Then."

"Anyway, I'm sorry."

"Or if you apologize again. Then."

"Sorry," Vanja said before she could stop herself.

Nina gave her a kick. "Last chance. Good night."

Vanja heard Nina's breaths deepen and slow down, heard the rustle of sheets when Nina's legs twitched as she drifted off. It shouldn't be that difficult to fall asleep; it had been a long day. The business with the suitcase had been draining, and she was used to sharing a bed. But the warmth radiating from Nina's back was so palpable. It spread down the backs of her legs and made the soles of her feet prickle. Vanja scooted as close as she could without actually touching Nina's back with her own. She lay awake for a long time.

THE SECOND WEEK

FIRSTDAY

Vanja woke on her back with Nina's breath on her cheek. As she opened her eyes, she caught Nina quickly closing hers. Nina lay on her side, hands cradled against her chest. One of her elbows touched Vanja's upper arm; a knee brushed against Vanja's thigh. The two points of contact burned her skin through the layers of clothes. Vanja closed her eyes again and lay very still. At length, Nina sighed and sat up. She slid down to the foot of the bed and onto the floor, where she hunted around for her socks.

"Sock, sock, shoe, shoe. Trousers, shirt," she mumbled at the garments as she picked them up. "Brr. Cold. Good morning!"

"Good morning." Vanja stretched. Her body ached, as if she'd been tensed up in her sleep.

Nina opened her wardrobe and took out a pair of boots. "Here, my spares." She placed them next to the bed.

"Thank you very much," Vanja mumbled.

"Keep them. It's better that someone's using them."

Vanja stayed in bed until Nina had finished dressing and gone down to the kitchen. She crawled out from under the blanket and picked up her neatly folded clothes from the desk chair. The boots were a size too big, but she could walk in them. Her arm and leg tingled where Nina's body had touched hers. If the new bed wasn't delivered today, they would have to share again tonight. At first she didn't recognize the sensation that flared in the pit of her stomach. It had been so long.

Ulla was in the kitchen, pouring a cup of dark and acrid-looking coffee. "Good morning." She gave Vanja a small smile.

"Good morning," Vanja replied.

"Had another accident, did you?" Ulla's smile became a strange grin.

"I'm sorry," Vanja said. "I really am."

Ulla tutted. "You're not in Essre anymore, dear."

"I know. I'm sorry."

"Don't apologize. It's done." Ulla paused. "What did it look like?"

"What did what look like?"

"When the suitcase had dissolved. What did it look like?"

Vanja shrugged. "It didn't look like much at all. Just . . . sludge."

"I thought you were a researcher."

"What do you mean?"

"I would expect some curiosity," Ulla said. "A good researcher is curious about everything. Even that which one would find terrifying."

"I'm curious," Vanja said. "But I wasn't going to stay there and watch."

"Well," Ulla said, "that's where you and I differ. I would have taken the chance to observe."

"Observe what?"

"How it behaves," Ulla said slowly.

Something in Ulla's eyes made Vanja shiver.

"Now, then," Ulla said in a very different voice, "did you want to interview me, too? Nina said you might want to talk to an old doctor."

"I'll let you know," Vanja said. "I have to go write a report."

"You do that," Ulla replied. "You know where to find me."

Finishing her next short report took some time because the memory of Nina's heat against her back kept distracting her, but finally it was done. Vanja put it in an envelope along with the first report. The box she'd brought from the pharmacy was just big enough to fit all the product samples and the envelope. It was also just about light enough that she could carry it on her own, so she did, to the post office next to the train station. The clerk informed her that the train from Essre was on its way in to load and unload and placed Vanja's parcel on one of the pallets headed for the platform.

Vanja stepped out onto the platform. The tracks ran in a straight line to the south until they climbed a low hill and disappeared. The train was on its way down that hill, and the rails gave off a whirring sound that made the hairs on Vanja's neck stand up. The noise rose in volume as the train approached; when the train finally arrived at the platform, it was so loud Vanja had to cover her ears. The train was made of good metal that had been in use ever since the pioneers arrived, scratched and eroded, painted over many times. A section of the paint on the passenger car had bubbled and come loose, as if exposed to extreme heat. It hadn't looked like that when Vanja had last seen it. Something must have happened out there. Everyone knew the world outside of the colonies was dangerous, but the committee had never spoken of the details. Vanja thought about herself in the little car, unaware of the world outside the train's protective shell, of whatever it was that could do something like this to a train made of good metal.

Amatka Children's House Three had one hundred and seventeen residents between the ages of six months and fifteen years. The principal, Larsbris' Olof, had no objections to Vanja's surprise visit; he was happy to show her through the building and tell her about their hygiene habits. The air in the residential area of the building was thick with the smell of vinyl mattresses and soap. It was bathing day. In the long sunken tubs in the basement, the children sat in rows, each scrubbing the back in front of them. Those at the end of a row had their backs scrubbed by an older sibling. It was always a race to not end up at the back of a row. Elders always scrubbed too hard, seeking revenge for all those times elders had bruised their backs when they were little.

"Atopic eczema, acne, dandruff," the principal said as he led Vanja back upstairs. "And fungal infections. That's what we deal with here. We could use something more effective against dandruff. The hair soap we have, it doesn't work—it just makes your scalp dry and itchy. It's probably made in Essre. You can tell they've never been here and have no idea what the climate is like. No offense."

Vanja laughed in the way that meant *the place I come from is terrible, isn't it.*

They continued on to the classrooms. In three halls, one for each age group, students sat on long benches facing the teacher's desk. From the doors of two of the halls, only the muted sound of a teacher droning out a lecture could be heard. But from the third came the sound of a choir. Children's House Three must have gifted students or a skilled teacher, because the harmonies drifting out through the chink in the door made Vanja's eyes prickle. They were singing a version of "The Pioneer Song" with a beat that had been slowed down to an almost leisurely pace. Leaning on a solid fourth voice, the third and second voices entwined in a dissonance that wasn't quite a dissonance, out of which the first voice rose up into bright notes that somehow entered through the ear and into the throat, constricting it. The pain didn't dissipate until Olof had led her around a corner and out of earshot.

She only half listened to Olof's account of the house kitchen and the hygiene routines observed there. When he was done, she thanked him for the tour and left. She chose a route that brought her by the classrooms. The singing had ceased. Even so, she stopped for a moment, in case they might start again. Instead, the door swung open, and thirty children in the oldest age bracket drifted out. They squabbled, let out adolescent howls, elbowed each other, and stared at Vanja. There was no sign that any of them had just been part of creating a sound so beautiful it hurt. Vanja set her course for home with a feeling of having somehow been made fun of.

———

That night, the bed still hadn't arrived. The four members of the household had dinner together; the conversation consisted mainly of Nina's small talk and Ulla's acerbic comments. Vanja replied mechanically to questions aimed at her. She caught herself avoiding Nina's eyes. Bedtime was very slow in coming. They undressed in silence. This time, Vanja carefully scooted back until one of her shoulder blades brushed against Nina's back. Nina didn't pull away, but nor did she come closer.

Report 2: Summary

Herein follows a summary of the observations, examinations, and interviews not included in report 1.

The employees of Amatka's clinic use the commune's own products exclusively. When asked about her opinion of products from other manufacturers, such as Amatka's First Independent Chemist, a senior physician replied that the products have not been available long enough to assess the effects of prolonged use. Therefore, the clinic administration has no interest in new products.

Employees at Amatka's mushroom farms have expressed a need for a milder laundry detergent. The fungicides in the detergent used for their protective clothing cause many farmers to develop rashes and flaking skin. The skin reactions can be treated with creams, but return as and when treatment stops. No other needs have been expressed.

My general impression continues to be that except in the case of the mushroom farmers, there's a sense of unease when discussing innovation and new products. Establishing anything but the commune's first products seems to have been a struggle. Introducing even newer ones might be very difficult. I will, however, continue my investigations.

With kind regards,
Brilars' Vanja Two

SECONDAY

The bookshelves in the library had been reorganized to make the gaps less obvious. Evgen sat behind his desk, writing index cards. When Vanja came in, he looked up and gave her a guarded smile. He looked less devastated.

"Hello again," Vanja said.

"Welcome back," Evgen said. "How are you getting on with number seven?"

"I like it very much."

"Keep it a while. It gets better every time you read it."

"I forgot to register it properly last time." Vanja put the book down on the desk.

"Right, right." Evgen took the library card from the pocket inside the cover and wrote something on it.

"Have you read any of her other poetry?" Vanja asked.

Evgen looked up. "What other poetry?"

Vanja hesitated. "I heard . . . I heard she wrote other poetry as well."

Evgen rubbed the library card between his fingers. "Nothing that's been published," he said eventually. "Except the hymn."

"A hymn?"

"Yes. But it's not considered part of her work." Evgen shrugged. "I can show it to you."

He walked over to a bookcase in a different part of the room and drew out a thin booklet. "Here."

The booklet was printed with the title *A Book of Songs by Amatka's Best Poets*. Evgen opened it, turned a couple of pages, and held it out to Vanja. It was a call-and-response chant.

We chose the committee	*to care for us*
We thank them	*for the gift of calm*
We thank them	*for their steady rule*
We thank them	*for telling us*
What to do	*what to do*
Thank you	*for your guidance.*

Vanja looked up at Evgen. "It seems . . . ," she started, "sarcastic?" Evgen gave her a tight smile.

An awkward silence descended on the room. Evgen seemed about to speak a few times but stopped himself.

"Listen," Vanja said finally, "I was wondering if you have any historical information on . . . on hygiene habits?"

Evgen blinked. "Hygiene?"

"Yes. Because I'm actually here on an assignment. For a hygiene company. And I thought that maybe you might have some books or documents about that kind of thing."

Evgen stared into space for a few seconds. Then he said "Hygiene, no, no books. But the letter collections." He stood up and walked around his desk, heading for a door at the far end of the room. "Follow me."

It was a long, narrow room, almost like a corridor. Shelves running the length of the walls were stacked with meticulous rows of gray boxes. Vanja walked along the shelves. The boxes weren't marked BOX. Their rough surfaces were only labeled with years and subject words.

"Where did these boxes come from?" she asked. "Are they . . . ?"

Evgen nodded. "Good boxes. They've been here from the start."

He pulled out a box and put it in Vanja's hands. "What's this?" Vanja locked her elbows to get a better grip.

"Letters and journals. Some people I came to think of."

"Do you know this archive by heart?"

Evgen reached for another box. "I sort all the documents that come in when someone's died. All biographical texts are to be preserved."

"But you haven't always been here, have you? How do you know so much about them?"

"I like reading." Evgen waved his box at the door.

He set his box down on the table in the middle of the library. Vanja put hers on top. Evgen took a pair of thin gloves from his pocket and handed them to her.

"Like I said, letters and journals," Evgen said, and opened the first box. "This one contains letters from one Kettuns' Daniel. He frequently wrote to his brother in Essre about some sort of eczema he had. His brother sent the letters here a couple of years ago, after Daniel's death." He pointed to the other box. "Journal entries and letters from pioneers in that one. Some of them mention, uh, bodily matters."

"Is this paper, all of it?" Vanja asked. "Good paper?"

"It is. And I won't let the committee have it." Evgen made a face. "Yet."

"That's good."

"There's coffee in my thermos," Evgen said. "In case you need it."

Vanja smiled at him. He returned the smile, warily, and sat back down at his desk. Then there was just the rasp of his pencil on the index cards.

Like Evgen had said, Kettuns' Daniel's letters were all addressed to a brother, Vikuns' Tor, in Essre. The oldest letter had been written ten years earlier; the last one was three years old. Daniel had written about one letter every other month and almost exclusively about his body.

Dear brother,

I hope you're well. Over here things have been a little rough lately. The eczema and all that is getting worse. I wash as little as I can and rub on rich creams but it keeps spreading. The doctor says it's not psoriasis but it sure looks like it to me. I've read about it at the library. Bathe less and keep moisturizing, that's what the doctor keeps telling me. I'm only supposed to take baths every other week and just wash with a cloth and soap for the rest. The doctor says the intimate soap is the best but I don't like the smell. Then I'm supposed to use the rich cream. I rub it in and rub it in but I just get kind of greasy. It just sits on top of the rash. Well, that's enough about that.

Vanja leafed through the pages. Detailed accounts of Daniel's hygiene habits, his opinions on various soaps and creams, his ruminations on himself. He never referred to his brother's replies. But the eczema grew steadily worse.

Well, I don't know what to do. Nothing's helping. That crusty eczema on the backs of my knees and on my back and in the crooks of my arms, they've spread to my scalp. The skin feels sort of brittle and it hurts when I touch it. The scurf on my scalp itch and run. The doctor says it could be a psychosomatic reaction. He means I'm a hysteric. He didn't say "hysteric" but I could hear that that's what he was thinking. He asked me how I was feeling. Fine, I said, except for the eczema. I don't want to go back there anymore. I feel so small when I have to show them all my defects and ailments. Like I'm whiny. I almost wish I had a broken leg or something because then at least there would be something properly wrong with me. Then they could say "you have a broken leg" and fix it.

Daniel tried a range of different treatments: he was committed to the clinic for a round of warm mushroom poultices. He tried diets that excluded mushrooms, root vegetables, or beans by turns. Nothing worked. His joints and muscles began to ache. He wrote less and less often.

I wake up too early in the morning and just lie there, not knowing what to do with myself. I think about when we were little and played by the railroad tracks. Do you remember when we put forks and knives on the rails and waited for the train to come flatten them? We waited all afternoon. No train in sight. We'd got the day wrong. But you talked about taking that train one day, all the way across the tundra to Essre, and becoming someone special there. I hope you've become someone special. I thought about something else, too. Another memory:

The rest of the letter was missing. Vanja leafed through the pages. The letter at the bottom of the box consisted of a few short lines. It was dated several months after the previous one.

Things are tough right now. I don't have a job anymore. They say I'm too ill to work. All I do is sit at home and look out the window. I think about you. Why haven't you replied?

"Excuse me," Vanja said out loud. "Do you know what happened to Daniel? Why he died? Because he didn't die from eczema, did he?"

"I remember it well," Evgen said from his desk. "He lay down in front of the auto train. People talked about it for months."

Vanja opened the next box, which contained documents from a number of authors. The paper was thin, some sheets were brittle. The documents smelled dry and musty at the same time. She leafed through logs, letters, a few journals. Most were letters. She had some success: letters from an engineer discussing the development of the commune's products with a colleague. A doctor ranting in his diary about the excessive use of soap. After a while, she noticed a cup of coffee by her elbow. The doctor's diary ended abruptly. The last third had been ripped out.

Some letters from a "Jenny" filled the bottom third of the box. Jenny was a pioneer—not just a pioneer to Amatka from Essre, but born on the other side, before the colonization. She wrote letters to her mother in a childish, sprawling hand.

Vanja learned in the first letter that Jenny's mother hadn't joined the colonization. Jenny wrote to her anyway, to keep the memory of her mother alive. She gave detailed descriptions of the colonization as she lived it: long rides on uncomfortable seats in coaches that broke down one after the other; the temporary camps; the "hard mental work" of building Amatka. After that particular mention, the page had simply been cut in half. When the letter continued, Jenny was complaining about the lack of basic necessities and that they had to go months without basic hygiene and medical supplies.

> I'm so tired of washing menstrual pads. I'm tired of the cloth pads and smelling people's bad breath. It would be so wonderful to wear a disposable pad just once, or—the luxury—a tampon! And to brush my teeth.

Vanja noted the word "disposable pad" down. Several pages were missing from this letter as well. Finally, she got up to stretch her back. There was a vague discomfort in her belly. She must be hungry.

"Did you find anything?" Evgen said from his desk.

"Yes, plenty. But there are pages missing in several places."

"That means they've been redacted."

"Redacted?"

Evgen cleared his throat. Vanja pulled the corners of her mouth down. Evgen looked at her and nodded. Silence fell once more.

"Is that your job?" Vanja asked.

"Yes. At least it is when new material comes in."

"So then you know what they said."

He cleared his throat again.

"Sometimes I think . . . ," Vanja began, glancing at Evgen.

If she had misinterpreted him the last time she was here, this could end badly. She steeled herself and continued. "Sometimes I think it would be nice to know if one could choose another way of life. If it were possible to find out what really happened before. And then make up one's own mind."

Evgen met her gaze. He was about to reply when the door slammed in the coatroom. He instantly started putting the papers back into the boxes. Vanja slunk out the door while the new visitor quizzed Evgen about biographies.

The bed hadn't arrived. They lay back-to-back. If Nina found it awkward, it didn't show. If she liked sharing the bed, that didn't show, either. Her studying Vanja that first morning had probably been a coincidence. Vanja lay awake feeling the warmth of Nina's body where it touched hers, trying to soothe herself by thinking about what she remembered from *About Plant House 7*.

There was something about Berols' Anna's language. It was as though she understood words and objects on a deeper level than anyone else. The poems weren't just simple marking rhymes or descriptions of the world. Vanja had a feeling that the plant houses didn't need marking anymore, because Berols' Anna's words had fixed their shape so completely.

THIRDAY

Again, Ulla opened the door immediately, as if she had been waiting on the other side. She showed Vanja into her room. "Take a seat," Ulla said. "I'll get you something to drink. Would be rude if I didn't."

Vanja waited while Ulla dug out a little bottle and two cups from her cabinet. At length, she sat down and poured the bottle's contents into the cups. It was wine, and it had a sour bouquet Vanja didn't recognize. "What is it?" she asked.

Ulla winked at her. "It's the good stuff. Go on, then, interview me."

"Right." Vanja picked up her notepad and pen. "Sarols' Ulla Three, retired doctor. Your speciality?"

"General practitioner," Ulla replied. "Retired fifteen years."

"And what do you do now?"

"Wait for death or better times."

Vanja looked up.

Ulla raised her cup and grinned. "That, and I rattle my pill organizer with the other decrepits at the recreation hall."

"So." Vanja cleared her throat. "You remember when new hygiene products were introduced?"

Ulla laughed. "Yes, hygiene products. All right. Yes, I remember.

We all thought it was silly. Everyone was using the commune's own, and then these two new companies came along. And there will be more, as I understand it. From Essre?"

"That's the idea."

"But there is no difference, you know." Ulla poured herself more wine. "New manufacturers, new labels. The muck they make it from is exactly the same."

"That's actually not true," Vanja ventured. "Among other things, extract of agaric is used in . . ."

"Extract of agahhhric," Ulla mimicked. "Oh really. And what's the main ingredient?"

"Well . . . soap base. And cream base."

Ulla raised an eyebrow. "And what's that made of? Because it's not all mushroom extracts and bean oils."

"It's . . ." Vanja struggled. "It comes from the factories in Odek."

"That's right." Ulla patted Vanja's hand. "And what do they manufacture in the factories in Odek? What is the substance they use to make every last thing we have?"

Vanja swallowed.

Ulla shot her a sharp smile. "Isn't it strange how one is so frightened by, say, a cup dissolving into sludge? And in the next moment, one rubs oneself all over with something that's made from exactly the same sludge."

"It's not the same," Vanja protested. "It's . . . a cream base. The other is . . . it's . . ."

"You know what it is. Everything that comes out of the factories is made from the same stuff."

It was almost as though the shape of the cup in front of her was starting to melt, as though the table were suddenly sagging.

"Table," Vanja mumbled reflexively. "Cup."

"Exactly!" Ulla said. "You know how it works. Everyone knows how it works."

"Why are you being like this?" There was a sour taste at the back of Vanja's throat.

The sharp smile returned. "Because I think it's funny. It's so funny that you can be so aware of the truth, and still come here and try to sound as though your . . . specialists, or whatever they are, that you're making something that doesn't come from the same place as every-thing else. Tables and cups. Creams and clothes and . . . suitcases." The last word was no more than a whisper.

"You said it yourself, everyone knows." Vanja pushed her chair back.

Ulla watched her with unblinking eyes. "But have you never won-dered?" she said. "If you just changed a consonant, or . . . misspoke. Just once." She pointed at Vanja's cup. "Knife," she hissed.

The word stabbed at Vanja's ears. She couldn't look away from the cup. It kept its shape.

Ulla laughed. "Look how scared you are!"

"I could . . . I could report you." Vanja got to her feet and moved away from the cup.

"Go ahead. Don't just stand there like an idiot. Go and make your report." Ulla reached for Vanja's cup and raised it to her lips. "But I don't think you will."

"Why not?"

Ulla looked at Vanja over the rim of her cup. "Because I think that someone who lets two of her things dissolve over the course of just one week . . . might not be too happy with the order of things, if you know what I mean." She slurped at her wine. "Besides, didn't you hear? I'm old and confused."

Vanja spent the afternoon in her room, wrapped in a duvet at her desk. All she could see through the window were roofs and the curves of the plant houses beyond. *About Plant House 7* lay opened in front of her, full of comforting descriptions of the world, more and more soothing every time she read them. And yet Ulla's words wouldn't leave her alone. *Someone who lets two of her things dissolve over the course of just one week might not be too happy with the order of things.* Neither was Ulla, it seemed. And if one were to judge from that hymn and handwritten poetry, nor was Berols' Anna. There was more to her than the plant house poems and the simple epitaph in the history book. Ulla knew something. She wanted something, too. The question was what.

FOURDAY

"Distillate Number One, forty-six volume percent alcohol. Made from turnips," Vanja read out loud.

"Amatka's most popular alcoholic beverage, after Distillate Number Four," Nina said. "Average consumption three point seventy-five liters per person per year."

"How do you know?"

"Because I have patients with cirrhosis. There's a lot of cirrhosis going around."

"In Essre, it's two and a half liters," Vanja said.

"And how do you know that?"

"I wrote a pamphlet about temperance." Vanja held out her cup.

Nina chortled and gave her a refill. It was the afternoon. It had been about an hour since Nina came home and set the bottle on the table with a deep thud: "I have tomorrow off. Let's drink."

And that was that. Nina made strong coffee and poured enough distillate in the cups that the rising steam pricked Vanja's nostrils. The liquor was harsher than in Essre and spread an acrid warmth through her chest. Nina was rosy cheeked and told stories about patients with weird injuries.

Vanja's shoulders were slowly lowering. She had no funny stories to tell, but she enjoyed listening to Nina.

"It's great seeing you laugh," Nina said.

Vanja flushed. "What, don't I normally?"

Nina shook her head. "No. And that's a shame, because your whole face lights up. You're so serious all the time, all worry lines."

Vanja scraped at the bottle's label with her thumbnail. "Maybe."

Nina reached out and stopped her fidgeting. "Hey. What happened to you?"

"What do you mean, what happened to me?"

"You know, when we were at the clinic. Down at the fert unit."

"Oh. That."

"Do you want to talk about it?"

"There's not much to say."

Nina took the bottle and mixed them a new batch of coffee and distillate. "It happened to me, too," she said. "Before I had Tora. Ivar and I had been inseminating at home, you know, with one of those baster things . . ."

"Inseminating?" Vanja said. "I thought you were . . ."

"What? No, no." Nina laughed. "Haven't you ever wondered why we have separate rooms?"

"I thought it was so there would be fewer empty rooms."

Nina laughed again and shook her head. "No, no, no. See, we're best friends since the children's house. We've always lived together. It was just more practical to make a couple of children together, instead of standing in line at the clinic or trying to pick someone up at the leisure center."

"I see." Vanja started picking at the bottle label again.

"Anyway . . . we'd been trying for a good while with that syringe. And then I thought it finally worked. But I had a miscarriage more or less straight away. It was horrible."

"But why?" Vanja said quietly. "Why was it horrible?"

"Because I'd been hoping, you know? And because I wanted to have children, and, well, contribute. Do my part for the commune. According to my ability, right?" Nina shrugged. "But then Tora and Ida came. I guess I'm trying to say that things might go better next time."

"There is no next time," Vanja said. She pinched a corner of the label between her thumb and forefinger and tugged at it. "They've given up. It didn't work."

Nina sighed. "I'm so very sorry to hear that."

Vanja tore the corner off and rolled it between her fingers. She downed her drink. "But that's not why."

"Then why?" Nina tilted her head.

"I mean. What if one doesn't want to." The words seemed to have a will of their own. "If one doesn't want to have children. One waits, and sort of hopes that it doesn't have to happen. And then one turns twenty-five, and the questions start coming, and they put you in a room with a counselor who explains that it's one's communal duty, and finally one gives in, one goes to the fert unit and shakes hands with some pitiful man who has to masturbate into a cup so the doctors have something to impregnate one with, and one resigns and puts one's feet in the stirrups because one has. No. Choice." She was out of words. She rested her face in her hands.

Nina got up from her chair and sat down next to Vanja. She pulled her close and held her without speaking.

After a while, Vanja straightened up. She wiped her face with her shirtsleeves.

Nina put a hand on Vanja's knee. "I'm sorry you're in pain, Vanja. I really am. But both you and I do know why everything is like it is. It's so that we can survive."

Vanja stood up. The room seemed to tilt sideways ever so slightly. "I'm going out."

She went up to her room and stuffed two blankets into her satchel. She looked into the kitchen on her way out. Nina sat with her chin in her hand. She was topping off her cup again.

The raw lake air was refreshing, even though everything still felt remote. Vanja walked north along the beach. Tundra, shingles, grass. She came to a spit of land where a group of boulders offered shelter from the wind and a place to sit. She spread out a blanket and sat down with her back to one of the larger rocks. Dusk was falling. Slow waves lapped against the beach; the rush of water on stone was unfamiliar and calming at the same time. Her eyes felt crusty from tears and alcohol. Vanja tied her earflaps under her chin, leaned her head back against the rock, and closed her eyes.

They were always kind. The doctors, the nurses, the technicians. It was always with the same polite care that they showed her to her room, established that it was time, examined her. A nurse held her hand and gently pushed her shoulders back into the chair when she panicked. They tried to comfort her, telling her that it was normal to be nervous, that she was such a good girl, while they attempted to plant a little parasite inside her.

The sound of footsteps made her open her eyes again. It had grown darker, and the waves had abated. A figure stood a few steps away. In the fading light, it was hard to make out features, but the posture made it look like an old woman in a pair of overalls. She was holding the end of something resembling a stick, or a pipe, which she'd plunged into the water. The woman turned. It was too murky to see her face. She nodded at Vanja and turned back toward the lake.

When the water whitened, the old woman raised her arms so that the end of what she was holding hung just below her chin. She supported her elbows on her stomach and remained standing like that while the water froze. Vanja tried to keep her eyes open, but the drowsiness was overpowering. She managed to raise her eyelids a couple of times. The woman was still there, unmoving.

When Vanja managed to open her eyes one last time, all she could see was the woman's silhouette against the light from Amatka's plant houses; the lake was a still, black expanse, inseparable from the night. The woman took a deep breath and put her lips to the thing she held in her hands. Vanja felt rather than heard the note vibrate through her body. It continued for a long time. Finally, the sound faded. The woman straightened and pulled the pipe up. It ended in a narrow funnel. The woman slung the pipe over her shoulder and left.

It was warm between the blankets. The rocks around her were comfortable if Vanja just adjusted her position a little. She leaned back, turned her head, and closed her eyes again.

It happened at dawn. Something like a chorus of discordant flutes rang out. Vanja turned her head. A group of people were approaching across the ice. She couldn't quite make them out; their shapes wavered as if in a heat haze. She was so tired. Her eyes fell shut again.

The beach bathed in the light of morning. She must have slept through the breaking of the ice. Her neck ached. When she stood up, the hangover hit her.

FIFDAY

Nina sat by the kitchen table with her head in her hands. If she'd been sitting there all night, or if she'd just sat back down, was impossible to say. The bottle and the cups were cleared away, in any case. She turned toward the door when Vanja entered.

"Where have you been?"

"By the lake."

"All night?"

"All night. I fell asleep."

"How stupid can you get?" Nina stood up. "You walk off just like that and don't come back. Do you think that's fair?" She was standing in front of Vanja now, gripping her shoulders. "And you can't just spend the night there. People have disappeared that way, Vanja."

Vanja looked down at her shoes. Nina let go of her shoulders and rubbed her face.

"I'm sorry," Vanja said. "I didn't know you'd be worried."

Nina lowered her hands and stared at Vanja. "You *are* stupid."

Vanja stared back. "I don't understand."

"Yeah, that much is clear." Nina took one of Vanja's hands in hers and trailed her fingertips over the red knuckles. "You're all chapped."

She abruptly let go and went into the bathroom. After rummaging around for a moment, she came back out, a jar in her hand. "Sit down."

Nina sat down next to her, opened the jar, and dipped a finger in it. She took one of Vanja's hands and rubbed cream into the knuckles with light, circular movements. Vanja's skin stung as the cream sank in. Nina's hands worked their way down her fingers. Where she touched the delicate fold between the fingers, little warm jolts traveled up Vanja's wrist. Her consciousness narrowed down into the point where their bodies met. Vanja extended her hand, and Nina's fingers wandered up to the thin skin on the inside of her wrist. She didn't dare look up.

Nina leaned over until their faces nearly touched, so close that Vanja felt the warmth radiating from her skin. Then her lips brushed the corner of Vanja's mouth. Just once, gently. She pulled back a little.

Vanja touched the spot where Nina had kissed her. It almost hurt. "I didn't think."

There were no more words. Instead, she leaned forward.

Later, when they lay curled up face-to-face in Nina's bed, and Nina's hand traced the contours of Vanja's face, the cuff of her sleeve tickling Vanja's cheek, Vanja said: "What do you dream about at night?"

Nina smiled weakly and ran her fingers through Vanja's hair. "Oh, you know. About Sevenday and playing with the girls. About going to work. Or about going to work naked." She raised her eyebrows. "Or about being naked with someone . . . like that shy beauty from Essre." She chuckled. "You're blushing!"

"No, I'm not."

Nina stopped laughing, but the corners of her mouth twitched. "I didn't mean to embarrass you."

Vanja smiled a little and shook her head. She made another attempt. "Have you ever dreamed about something that doesn't, I mean, that doesn't belong here?"

Nina stiffened. "Why would you ask me that?"

"I was just wondering."

Nina rolled over onto her back. She stared at the ceiling.

"I think everyone has," Vanja said. "Sometime."

"I don't understand why you want to talk about it."

Vanja hesitated. "Not sure."

Nina glanced at her. She extended an arm and pointed at the poster on the wall. *As morning comes we see and say: today's the same as yesterday.* "Today's the same as yesterday," she said.

"Today's the same as yesterday," Vanja echoed.

"Full stop." Nina rolled back onto her side and pulled Vanja toward her. She was solid, tangible. Vanja sank into her spicy-sweet scent.

The slam of the front door woke her. She glanced at the clock. It was almost three. Beside her, Nina stretched languidly.

"I have to go," Vanja said. "I have to make a telephone call at four."

"To whom? Your supervisor?"

Vanja nodded. "It's some sort of debriefing. I'm supposed to get new assignments for the final week . . ." She paused. "This is my final week."

Nina slid an arm around her waist. "Stay a while longer," she mumbled into Vanja's neck.

"I really have to be there at four."

"No, I mean stay here. Quit that job. Stay here with me."

"Is that what you want?"

"I just told you."

Vanja sat up. "I need to think."

"I don't like the sound of that." Nina pulled her arm back.

"No, I mean . . ." Vanja picked at the cuff of her shirt. "I need to think."

"I'll try not to worry while you do, then. Off you go."

———

Vanja walked in a slow spiral through the streets toward the center. Soon, she would board the train and go home. Everything would be just like before, the days lined up in perfect uniformity: she would go to work, go home, go to bed. She would go to the leisure center on Sevendays and watch the others play games and dance; day after day after day, just like she always had, until she retired and moved into the home for the elderly to await death. Without Nina.

At five minutes to four, as she stood at the commune office's reception desk with a large, black telephone in front of her, she had made up her mind. She read the wall posters while the receptionist shuffled papers on the other side of the desk.

"It's four o'clock," the receptionist eventually said.

He picked up the receiver, pressed a button, and handed the receiver to Vanja.

The supervisor's voice was faint and crackly on the other end of the line. She was very impressed with Vanja's work so far, and would send her extra credits as a reward. She looked forward to seeing Vanja do a presentation when she returned to Essre. Vanja's work was so outstanding it would be used as a model for future market research. And would she be interested in going to Odek or Balbit after this? Or would she prefer to stay in Essre?

"No," Vanja said carefully. It felt right. "No. I'm going to stay here."

"But you can't do that," the supervisor said. "You were supposed to give a presentation. That's part of the assignment."

"That's not in my contract. It says I'm supposed to collect and send information."

"No, but of course you're supposed to present it, too. We have to be able to ask questions!"

"Everything is in the reports. There's not much else. I'll send the final report soon."

The line crackled empty for a moment. "I don't know what to say," the supervisor said eventually. "I didn't see this coming."

"My contract doesn't state," Vanja repeated, "that I'm supposed to do more than conduct an investigation and then send you reports."

"But it's a given."

"Not to me. And it doesn't say how long I have to work for, either. You only said to take all the time I needed. And I have."

"I see." The supervisor's voice was strangely small. "You do understand that you're making our job harder, Vanja. What we're trying to do is no easy thing."

"Well, be that as it may, I'm resigning."

"You'll lose your bonus." The voice had slipped into a whine. "And I won't write a letter of recommendation."

"It's just soap. Good-bye," Vanja said.

"Shit," the supervisor said.

Vanja put the receiver down. She let out a long, shuddering breath.

The receptionist lifted the telephone off the desk and looked at her with raised eyebrows. He had very obviously listened in on the conversation.

"I'm registering for residence." Vanja took her papers out of the breast pocket on her anorak. "And I want to sign up for work."

Becoming a member of Amatka's commune was a quick process. A short form to complete the information she had given on arrival, a requisition form for transport of any belongings from Essre, a labor registration form where she listed her skills and work history. The receptionist took the finished forms, read them through, and then dug a list out of one of the piles of paper on the desk. He checked Vanja's labor registration form against the list, nodded, scrutinized her, and then looked back down at the papers.

"You'll be an assistant here at the commune office," he said. "That's what's available. Because I noticed you have no farming experience."

"No."

"You'll start on Firstday at eight, work until five, one-hour break at midday."

"What will I be doing?"

"Admin tasks. We'll go through them when you start. I'm busy at the moment."

The receptionist sat back down behind the desk and demonstratively turned his gaze to his piles of paper.

Vanja stepped out onto the darkening plaza with a gnawing feeling in her stomach. Maybe this was all wrong. Maybe it was completely insane. She walked along the twilit streets, following the weary stream of workers on their way home. The outdoor lamps lit up one after the other. The cold yellow light brought out lines and folds in the introverted faces around her. No one met her gaze.

When she arrived at the household—no, home—the front door opened a crack. Nina stood in the coatroom, arms folded across her chest. She had been waiting. Vanja felt her face break into a smile. Nina smiled back, at first warily, then broadly.

"You're staying," she said when Vanja reached the door.

Something in Vanja's belly clenched hard and then relaxed. She nodded.

SIXDAY

Vanja sat at her desk wrapped in the duvet. She finished her last report, in which she noted that the citizens of Amatka had expressed no need for new hygiene products, with two exceptions: a hypoallergenic laundry detergent and a mild antidandruff hair soap. She ended the report with her resignation.

She looked at the report she had just written, stood up, took a turn around the room, and sat back down. The duvet bunched up under her thighs. There wasn't really anything else to say. She stared at her notes from the meeting with Ulla. They were unusable. They should be scrapped immediately. Instead, she put them at the very back of the NOTES folder. She gathered up the pages of the official report and popped them into a brown envelope. It wasn't even midday. She stared blankly at the envelope until the lumpy duvet under her legs brought her back, and she had to stand up and smooth it out. A small noise made her turn around. Tora and Ida stood in the doorway, watching her. It was impossible to tell how long they'd been standing there. Tora's shirt had food stains. Ida's mouth hung open.

Vanja attempted a smile. "Hello."

Without a word, they turned and ran.

———

Ivar was the one who had fetched the children. Vanja heard him pottering about in the kitchen, talking to them. Ulla was down there as well; the sound of her sharp voice carried up through the stairwell, but Vanja couldn't hear the actual words. Vanja waited until Ulla had shuffled back up to her own room, then went downstairs.

Ivar was frying something or other he'd found in the fridge. The children sat at the table, whispering to each other. They fell silent when Vanja entered.

Ivar turned halfway around. "I heard you're staying."

"Yes." Vanja hesitated in the doorway. She couldn't tell what Ivar was thinking.

Ivar turned back to the frying pan and nodded. "That's good. Nina will be happy."

"Oh. Good." Vanja stayed in the doorway.

Tora and Ida resumed their whispering.

"Could you make some coffee," Ivar said after a while.

They ate in silence. Vanja washed the dishes, then went upstairs. After some hesitation, she knocked on Ulla's door. This time, it took some time before Ulla opened. She looked tired and worn; her usual smile was gone.

"What?" she said.

"I need to ask you a question," Vanja said. "Can I come in?"

"Certainly." Ulla took a couple of steps back.

Inside, Vanja lowered her voice to a whisper. "Were you at the lake last night?"

Ulla raised an eyebrow. "Where does this come from?"

"I was there," Vanja said.

Ulla's smile returned. "Went down to the lake at night, did we?"

"I thought I saw someone who looked like you."

"I heard you were drinking."

"I was."

Ulla nodded. "So you went out to the lake, alone, drunk. What did you see exactly?"

"Um," Vanja said. "I saw someone . . . sticking a pipe into the water . . . and blowing into it. There was a noise."

"You realize how all this sounds, don't you?" Ulla smiled at her.

Vanja held her gaze. "I think that was you."

"And why would I be doing that?"

"Someone came from across the lake."

Ulla's eyes brightened for a moment. "Is that so?"

"Who was it?"

For a moment, Ulla looked as if she was about to say something. Then she shook her head. "You're very curious, my dear. And very reckless. I think you need to ask yourself what you're doing."

"So there was someone."

"I think maybe you need to stay sober." Ulla winked at her. "Now off you go."

Vanja returned to her room and stayed there until Nina knocked on the door to ask for help with dinner. Ulla was at the kitchen table, talking to the children. She grinned broadly at Vanja.

Someone eventually showed up to deliver a new bed. Vanja slept in her own room that night. Nina shared her bed with one of the girls. Vanja woke up several times, fumbling in vain for Nina's warmth. The new bed had a sharp factory smell. She rested her nose on the sleeve of her sleep shirt and breathed in the scent it had absorbed from Nina. It helped, a little.

SEVENDAY

Vanja accompanied Nina and Ivar to the leisure center. Nina and Ivar joined a ring dance with the girls. Before long, half of the people in there were dancing in a long, winding line, led by a man in a wheelchair who zigzagged his way through the hall. Those who weren't dancing clapped their hands to the rhythm and sang along in the chorus. Vanja stood at the back wall, behind the last row of benches. The din of the crowd was an assault on her ears. When someone suddenly tapped her shoulder, she jumped. It was Evgen. He leaned in close and cupped his hand around her ear. "It's nice to bump into you. How are you?"

"I'm fine, actually," Vanja yelled back. Raising her voice hurt her throat a little.

"And your research?"

"Well, yes. That's fine, too, but I'm quitting."

Evgen frowned.

"I mean, I'm quitting and I'm staying here," Vanja said. "I got a job."

"You got what?" Evgen leaned in closer.

"A job! At the commune office! Administration!"

Evgen put a hand on Vanja's arm and steered her closer to the exit, where the noise was less deafening. "Did you say you were going to do admin work?"

"In the reception. Sorting papers and filing and such."

Evgen squeezed his lips together and looked intently at her. Then he came closer again, his face turned toward the dancers so that he seemed to be commenting on the party. "Listen. What you said, the last time you came to the library."

Vanja nodded and smiled at the room.

"Maybe I can show you something. If you help me in return."

"With what?"

"You said it yourself. You'll be doing admin."

Evgen shifted uncomfortably where he stood and rubbed his hands together. "All right," he said after a moment's silence. "When it gets dark, go down to the lake. I'll meet you there."

"Tonight?"

"Tonight. When everyone's busy." He abruptly turned and left.

Vanja lingered. She even joined in a couple of ring dances. When dinner was served on the long tables, she made her excuses to Nina. She was tired, too many people. Nina smiled, gave her a long kiss, and left with her daughters to sit at one of the tables. The eldest girl looked over her shoulder at Vanja, and for the first time she took her mother's hand.

The remains of Old Amatka stood to the south, at the waterline: parts of the central building jutted out of the black ice, an angular husk that for some reason hadn't been dismantled.

Evgen had met her by the beach, and they had walked off toward the ruin in silence. Just outside the building, he stopped short. He was buttoned into an enormous overcoat with a thick collar. His face was framed by a brown hat with earflaps. Vanja looked around. He might of course have led her down here to cajole a confession out of her.

"What is it?"

Evgen looked over her shoulder and back at her. "Did you . . ."

"No, but." Vanja squinted at the darkness inside the ruin. She thought she could see something move in the doorway.

"Vanja." Evgen's voice was taut. "I've decided to trust you, because you're the first person I've met in a long time who's said anything close to what you told me in the library. Maybe you're just out to report me, but I . . . I'm willing to take the risk." He paused for breath. "If you don't know what I'm talking about, or if you're the least bit uncertain, then I want you to leave and this never happened. And if you report me, I'll report you."

The rest of the air escaped him with a sigh. He looked small where he stood against the weak light from the colony. After a moment, Vanja realized that he was as scared as she was, if not more. She took off one of her mittens and held out her hand. After a moment's hesitation he pulled off his glove and took it. His palm was moist and hot.

"Good." Evgen withdrew his hand and pulled out a couple of flashlights from his coat. He gave one to Vanja. "Let's go."

The doorway was partly buried in the ice, and they had to crouch to get through it. The room on the other side was perhaps thirteen by thirteen feet and completely bare. Vanja let the beam of her flashlight sweep across the walls. Flakes of green paint still clung to the rough surface.

"This was the reception," Evgen said.

Here and there, scraps of posters were stuck to the walls. There was no text, only images: a head in profile, a clenched fist, yellow rays over a landscape. Vanja aimed the beam at her feet. The ice was perfectly clear; she could see the floor a foot and a half below, bare save for a few scattered pebbles.

Further back there was another doorway, blocked with debris from a collapsed ceiling. Next to it, a set of stairs led up to the next floor. Evgen started to climb them. Vanja followed.

The construction—or deconstruction—had halted at the second floor. From the landing at the top of the stairs, two unfinished corridors led off in either direction. The left one had collapsed in on itself. Below, Vanja could glimpse the nearly buried door to the reception.

Evgen walked into the corridor on their right, stopping after a few feet. "Careful here. There's no floor."

Vanja walked up to stand next to him. The floor ended in darkness. She angled her flashlight downward. Below them lay the rest of the ground floor, what would have been the lounge next to the reception, if the building conformed to the standard layout. Evgen sat down on the edge and slid forward and down.

As Vanja peeked over the edge, she saw him climb down the pile of debris from the collapsed floor. She followed. The stack of thick slabs seemed stable. Evgen waited for her on the ice. He waved at her and walked around the pile to the other side. There was another doorway, half-hidden by rubble. Evgen shoved a lump of concrete aside and crawled in on his hands and knees.

He backed out again with a box in his hands. It looked like one of the boxes from the library archive. He put it down on the ice and sat down on the lump of concrete he'd just pushed away. "Have a seat."

Vanja sat down on the edge of a piece of collapsed floor. "Doesn't anyone else come here?"

Evgen shook his head. "It's too close to the water. People are afraid of the lake." He took the lid off the box and put it to one side. "Only the eccentric and the suicidal go down to the lake." Inside the box was another lid, which he also opened. He pushed the box toward Vanja. "These should have been given to the committee for destruction, but I couldn't do it."

It was full of good paper, most of it covered in handwriting. Vanja took her mittens off and picked up the topmost sheet. The paper was delicate, but the words were clear in the torchlight.

Would you believe it, mother. We've begun to see cats in the street. Cats and a couple of dogs. It's funny. They said they haven't found any animals in this world, at least nothing bigger than insects. But I thought I heard cat noises in the kitchen the other day. I

admit I've been thinking about her a lot lately. I wrote a little
story about her and drew some pictures. It's so strange that there
are no animals here. It feels empty.

Vanja recognized the childish handwriting. It was the rest of the
letter from Jenny, the girl who wrote about her longing for disposable
pads. The part Evgen had told her had been culled.

"Cats," Vanja said. "Dogs . . . what are they?"

"Animals. A type of organism, fairly large." Evgen gestured at
knee height. "In the old world, they were kept as companions. People
would eat some of them."

Vanja shuddered at the thought. "So they brought those? It says
she saw them in the street."

Evgen shook his head. "The pioneers didn't bring any animals
at all, I know that much. I've read somewhere that they had plans
to bring animals later, but it never happened. Something prevented
them."

"But if they didn't bring any animals . . ."

Evgen looked at her in silence. He pointed at the letter.

I had been dreaming about the time we spayed Sascha, and she
hid behind the sofa in the living room for two weeks. I woke up
because there was a noise from the kitchen: a faint knocking, and
then a scraping sound, over and over. Tock rasp, tock rasp.

I got out of bed. Raul was still sleeping. I went out into the
kitchen. It was Sascha. I would have recognized her anywhere—
her thin, crooked little body, her bow legs, her fur that always
looked dusty. She was wearing the cone. She was straining with
the cone against a kitchen cabinet, as if she was trying to wriggle
free of it. Then the cone slipped across the cabinet door. Rasp.
Sascha got up again and drove the cone into the cabinet: tock.

I called for her. Come here Sascha, come here sweetie, *I said.*
And she turned her head and looked at me. Then she meowed.

Do you remembered how Sascha had such a ridiculous voice?
She sounded like a squeaky toy when she meowed. She was so tiny

and crooked and grumpy. She was really not a very nice cat. But it was just because she was such a little runt that I couldn't help but love her. We belonged together that way, somehow. Do you remember how she was always at the bottom of the pecking order in the yard? She was allowed on the compost heap and under the dumpster. Everything else was claimed by the other cats. She'd sit there on the compost heap and chase flies. She'd never let you pet her. But sometimes, if you sat very still for a long time and pretended she wasn't there, she would slink over and curl up in your lap.

I'm stalling. The thing that happened in the kitchen. I suppose nothing actually happened. I called for her, and she turned around, and she made a sound. It didn't sound like a cat. It was a sort of bleat, like a sheep, no that's not a good description, but it's as close as I can get. It wasn't a cat sound. It wasn't Sascha, it wasn't a cat at all.

Vanja turned the paper over, but the other side was blank. If there were more pages, they were missing. "What was it?" she asked.

"The animal?"

"Yes."

Evgen gave her a long look. "I think you know."

Vanja folded the paper. Her hands were trembling.

"Read more." Evgen browsed through the pile and pulled something out. "Here. It's by an industrial inspector."

They were pages torn from a book, a log.

Upon arrival, the controller had immediately gone to the factory's employee quarters. He didn't look at the employee log, explaining that he usually didn't read it until bedtime. Apparently the controllers use the log to leave messages for each other. The controller had cooked himself a dinner consisting of preserves from the storage. He then made a preliminary examination of the factory in preparation for the main inspection next morning.

According to the controller, everything initially appeared to be in order. The assembly line started at one end of the factory, where the raw material was poured into the blender. The finished product was packaged at the other end of the factory, a hundred yards away.

When I asked the controller if anything in particular had raised his suspicions, he replied that the sound of the factory was different. Strange noises came from a source the controller was unable to identify. He said: "They sounded like little squeals." The controller went through the factory and checked the different stations. After some time, he realized the noise emanated from the conveyor belt.

He "stood at the end of the belt, where finished tubes were packed into boxes for transport. They wouldn't lie still in their boxes. All the tubes, containing Facial Cream #3, were emitting faint little squeals. There was a louder noise coming from the tanks containing the paste that was about to be poured into molds. Every time the paste was squeezed into the tubes, I heard a howl."

The controller followed the emergency protocol: he shut down production immediately, sealed the factory doors, and telephoned the office to alert them to the incident.

It was in the employee log that we found out what had caused the malfunction: the controller who had visited a week earlier to restock the preserves in the employee quarters. The pages in the log were filled with made-up, bizarre observations of the factory and the repeated claim that the machines were alive and wanted to procreate.

The products were scrapped and the factory quarantined. This is not an unusual event, and according to the commune office a year should be enough for conditions to settle. After that, production can resume as normal. Until then we will be using another factory in the vicinity.

Vanja put the papers back in the box. There was a sour taste on her tongue.

"I was on the committee a few years back," Evgen said. "I was deposed. It's a long story, but in any case, they offered me to resign voluntarily in exchange for a job at the library. I was entrusted with the task of redacting the archive material." He gestured at the box. "I should have scrapped it. And I did, at first. But then I couldn't do it anymore. I wanted to know." He looked up at Vanja. "Now I've entrusted this to you. You want to know. So few people want to know."

Vanja sat in silence, staring at the box. Her hands were freezing. She shoved them into the sleeves of her anorak. "We're the ones creating everything. Everything."

"They pump the raw sludge out of the ground over in Odek," Evgen said. "And then shape it in the factories."

"And we have to keep telling it what it is. Or it'll revert to sludge."

"But it's not just that. That . . . cat . . . came from somewhere."

"They talked it into existence."

"Just like Colony Five talked itself into destruction. . . ."

Vanja felt slightly sick at the thought of it.

"It doesn't have to be a bad thing," Evgen continued. "If we could harness it. Or if we could somehow live in harmony with it." He pointed at the papers. "It all starts with us forcing matter into a shape it can't maintain. If we didn't, if we could learn to live another way . . . But we can't, as long as all this knowledge is kept secret."

Evgen put the inner lid back on, then the outer one. "I don't know how much you've heard, but fifteen years ago we lost almost a hundred people."

"The fire in the leisure center?"

"There was no fire. It was Berols' Anna. The poet with the *Plant House* series. She left with a group of followers to start a new colony."

"What happened?"

"I don't know. They sent out a rescue team after a while. Officially, the rescue team found everyone dead, and then the story changed again—no one had ever left. Not even the members of the committee found out what had happened. Only the rescue team and the Speaker at the time knew, but he's dead now. Anyway, I think it's the other way around. I think Anna's people managed to create something new. Real freedom."

"What makes you think that?"

"They never brought any bodies back. They said they'd dug a mass grave out there, but I don't believe it for a second. Nobody would leave a hundred bodies out there when they could be recycled. We could never afford it." Evgen let out a long breath. "And I think, now that the committee is coming after the library . . . I think something is happening up here. Something big. I think the committee's afraid that whatever happened with Berols' Anna's people will happen here, too."

"They need the good paper for something."

"Yes, exactly. It's for documents and books, after all, for things that mark. That define. And they need lots of it. I've never seen anything like it."

"Can't you find out?"

"Hardly. I'm not on the committee anymore. But you could. You'll be able to go through the archives. You'll be able to find out what they want with all the paper."

"And if I can find that out . . ."

". . . then we can figure out what they're planning."

Evgen looked Vanja in the eye. "And you can help me find information about what happened with Anna's colony. Because if they succeeded, we have to learn how to do it. So we can do more than just survive. I mean, the way things are now—we're alive, but what kind of life is it?"

"We speak of new worlds, we speak of new lives, we speak to give ourselves, to become," Vanja mumbled.

"What's that?" Evgen said.

"It's a poem," Vanja said. "By Berols' Anna."

"I'm not familiar with that."

"It was in a book I found at Ulla's apartment."

"Huh," Evgen said. "I'd like to read that."

"You would have to speak to Ulla."

"Who is this Ulla?"

"A retired doctor," Vanja said. "She says she knew Anna back in the day."

"That's very interesting," Evgen said. "You should talk to her more."

"I am," Vanja said.

"What has she said?"

Vanja hesitated. "I'm not sure."

Evgen studied her. "Get back to me when you're sure, then."

The house was quiet and empty when Vanja returned. Ivar and Nina would come home alone; the children were always fetched from the rec center on Sevenday evening so they could start the week in their own beds at the children's houses. Vanja crawled into Nina's bed and lay awake until she heard footsteps on the stairs. Nina came into the room, moving as quietly as she could. Vanja heard clothes fall to the floor. Then Nina crawled in under the duvet. She slid an arm around Vanja's waist. Her touch spread warmth through Vanja's limbs, relaxing her tense muscles.

When Vanja decided to find the place outside Essre that Lars had told her about, she'd walked eastward for what felt like hours. At first the plant-house ring lit the ground before her, but the light soon began to fade. Instead, a cold gleam appeared up ahead. The ground slowly rose into a ridge that glittered with night dew in the backlight. From the top, the ground sloped sharply down into a deep valley. And there it was: the village.

Surrounded by a low wall, the windowless houses were irregularly shaped, rounded and flowing, their domed roofs crowned with little symbols. Among the buildings spotlights mounted on tripods illuminated patches of walls and ground. Vanja could make out figures moving about. They looked small at first, like children, until she realized that it was because the houses were enormous. The thresholds reached the people walking around outside to their knees. Some of the houses seemed to have soft walls that draped into folds, but seeing a figure in overalls leaning against one of them, Vanja realized they were hard, too.

She crept closer to see better. None of the people walking around among the buildings seemed to pay much attention to their surroundings. No one seemed to be standing watch. Vanja crawled through the cold grass until she could crouch behind the wall and peek over the edge.

The men and women wore torn and dirty overalls. The men's beards were unkempt, some long enough to reach their chests. They ambled aimlessly through the alleys or sat on the ground. No one spoke. Vanja jumped when a woman slowly turned her way and came closer. She waited for the woman to speak to her, or point and call out, or grab her. None of those things happened. The woman gawped at Vanja. Her black hair was dull and lank against her face. A thin string of saliva slowly dribbled down her chin and dripped onto her chest. Then her gaze moved on. She walked away.

Vanja crept along the wall, now and then peering over the top. It was the same everywhere: men and women silently and aimlessly shuffling about or leaning against the walls. The houses had no doors, just empty openings through which Vanja could glimpse beds and tables.

A man stepped out of one of the houses and into the light of a lamp. His overalls weren't as soiled as the others, and his beard still fairly tidy. Vanja didn't recognize him at first: his face was slack and expressionless, his eyes dry and lifeless. He was swaying. A dark stain slowly spread from his crotch down his legs.

Vanja ran back up the slope, away from the town and away from Lars, who wasn't Lars anymore.

THE THIRD WEEK

FIRSTDAY

Vanja presented herself at the commune office at eight o'clock on Firstday morning. She was greeted by the gangly man in the reception, who introduced himself as Heddus' Anders. He gave her a rundown of her tasks. He didn't seem especially delighted with her presence. "You got this job because it was the most highly prioritized position you're qualified for." Anders pursed his lips. "And we have to follow the priority order."

Vanja's new job consisted of sorting and filing processed applications, reports, and certificates. Every change in a citizen's life entailed paperwork: birth, relocation to the children's house, relocation to a household, education, procreation, work, retirement, death. All work-related events had to be documented as well, of course: employment, resignation, production, results, accidents. The never-ending stream of paper was ferried back and forth by the couriers out of the distribution hub next door. Being a courier was an envied position, reserved for disciplined youngsters in peak physical shape, model specimens of humanity who usually went on to occupy coveted positions at the commune office and on the committee.

Most forms originated in the clinic, the children's houses, the mushroom chambers, and departments inside the commune office. At the administration office, these were sorted, counted, and indexed, and the information they contained incorporated into the colony's statistics. Very important papers, such as birth certificates, were copied onto good paper.

At midday, Anders showed Vanja to the commune office's canteen, where stewed parsnip and some sort of agaric was on the menu. Anders sat down at a table together with a woman and two men from somewhere else in the office building. Vanja sat down next to him, was introduced to the others and then promptly ignored. It was a relief to be able to eat without having to make small talk. The others were busy discussing the imminent committee election: Who were the candidates? Who made a fool of themselves trying to get elected? Who looked like a promising choice? It eventually emerged that Anders was planning to run. Vanja wondered to herself what the others would say about him when they were out of earshot—that he was a suitable candidate, or that he was a moron.

In the afternoon, Anders put the box of forms she had gone through that morning in Vanja's hands and led her to the back of the office, where he opened a gray door. Vanja followed him down a set of stairs and into a long room lined with filing cabinets. The only break in the long rows was another door, marked only with the sign DOOR. Documents concerning citizens were stored in the cabinets to the left, documents relating to the colony's administration to the right. Vanja's task was to sort citizens' forms into the correct personal files.

"What's in there?" Vanja nodded at the other door.

"The secure archive," Anders replied curtly.

"What's that?"

"That's none of our concern." He pulled out a drawer in one of the general filing cabinets. It was nearly three feet deep.

Vanja pressed her lips together and began sorting forms into files. The personal files were all identical: a birth certificate, a graduation certificate, and so on and so forth. The supply of good paper was finite, however. Upon a citizen's death, their whole file was removed and pulped or scraped clean, and their name added to the list of the dead. All that remained of a citizen was a name, birth and death dates, profession, and cause of death. There was one death certificate among today's papers. Vanja removed the corresponding file—Anmirs' Anna Three—then opened the drawer that contained the records of the dead. It was divided into alphabetical slots, each with a list of names. Out of curiosity, she peeked behind the B label. Almost at the top of the most recent list sat the name: Berols' Anna Two, farming technician and poet. Cause of death: accident. She had been forty-three. Her date of death corresponded to the date of the fire at the recreation center.

When Vanja was done sorting the forms, Anders handed her a new stack; this time it was temporary documents that needed copying onto fresh mycopaper while they waited to be processed. This pile was thicker than the one that had arrived in the morning and kept Vanja busy for the rest of the afternoon, with only one short coffee break. At four o'clock, Vanja started home with fingers made white and dry from handling all that paper. That night, she had a completely normal dream: she sorted forms.

SECONDAY

At the midday meal on Seconday, the canteen was buzzing with conversation. Vanja sat down next to Anders and the colleagues who had ignored her the day before. ". . . five of them," one of the men said, the thin one who was so tall he had to hunch down over the table. He turned to Anders. "I'm sure you know more! The reports must have come in by now."

Anders shook his head. "I've no idea what you're talking about."

"Accident in the mushroom farm," said the woman. Her eyes showed a little too much white. "They say one of the tunnels collapsed."

"Well." Anders stuck his fork in a fried mushroom cap. "Nothing's come in."

"It will," the woman replied. "I heard it from someone who was there. I saw her in the street just an hour ago. Her face was completely white. Your colleague looks a little peaky too, by the way."

Anders poked Vanja's arm. "What's the matter with you?"

Vanja shook her head. The bite of food she'd just taken sat in a dry lump against the roof of her mouth. She forced it down. "I have a housemate down there."

The woman snorted. "Everyone has friends down there. Get a grip."

An older woman in neat overalls and a neck covered in mushroom farmer's eczema waited by the front desk. She was holding a sheet of paper. Anders shooed Vanja toward the pile of forms she hadn't managed to finish yesterday and turned to the farmer. It looked like they were comparing forms. Vanja strained to hear their conversation, but they were speaking too quietly.

When the farmer had left, Anders posted a short list of names on the wall. "Five farmers are missing," he said. "We have to get word out to their households. I'll go talk to the junior secretary."

Vanja scanned the list. The second name from the top was Jonids' Ivar Four.

Vanja and Nina sat at the kitchen table with a rapidly cooling evening meal between them. Vanja hadn't been allowed to go home and tell Nina herself. Everything had to be done according to protocol. Anders had sent a courier to inform the households of the missing workers. Toward the end of the day, the courier had returned to the office and informed Vanja that her housemate was missing. It was almost enough to make her laugh.

When the workday was finally over, Vanja went home to find Nina at the kitchen table and Ulla pacing the room with a look of either fear or excitement on her face. Nina had finally asked Ulla to stand still or leave, and Ulla had walked out into the fading afternoon light. Vanja had made a quick stew that neither one of them had touched. Nina sat with the tip of her thumb between her teeth, slowly chewing the nail down to the quick.

It was very late when the door opened to reveal Ivar, leaning against the doorjamb. He had washed his face, but his forehead was black around the hairline, his curly hair matted with dust. He was wearing someone else's coat. Nina rushed over to him and took him in her arms. He leaned his head on her shoulder and closed his eyes.

After a moment, Nina took a step back, bent down slightly to look him in the eye, and put a hand on his cheek. "Are you hurt? Do you feel sick?"

Ivar shook his head. "They've already checked me. All that's wrong with me is a scrape on my hand."

He let Nina steer him to a chair, slumped down on it, and stared at the wall. Nina filled a cup with water and placed it in front of him. He emptied it in one gulp and rested his head in his hands.

Nina put a hand on the back of his neck. "What happened?"

It took a while before he answered. "One of the chambers collapsed. The one with the cave polypores. The floor just fell away."

Nina moved her hands to his shoulders. "Were you hurt?"

"No, no," Ivar replied in a muted voice. "I already said. Could I have something to eat?"

Vanja reheated the evening meal and put a bottle of liquor on the table. Ivar shoveled food into his mouth and swallowed almost without chewing. The others waited until he pushed the empty plate away. He rested his head in his hands again.

"The floor caved in," he muttered between his fingers. "I fell through with it. It was a long way down. I landed on my back, had the air knocked out of me. Got covered in dirt." He rubbed at his eyes and looked up at Vanja and Nina. "Torun and Viktor were standing next to me when it happened. They just disappeared. I couldn't hear them. The others say I'm the only one who made it out."

Ivar poured liquor into his cup. His trembling hands made the bottle clatter against the rim. "There are tunnels. Under the mushroom farm. I don't know how long I was down there. What time is it?"

Vanja told him. Ivar nodded. He drained the cup, then filled it back up. He stared at the bottle. The muscles of his jaw flexed under his skin. "Somehow I was still wearing my headlamp," he said suddenly. "So I could see there was no way back up. The whole tunnel behind me was filled with debris. So I thought I'd try to find another way out. I couldn't see very far, but it was a big place. High ceiling. The walls and the floor were made of some sort of stone that sparkled. It was smooth, smoother than concrete. Maybe the others hit their heads on the floor, maybe that's why they haven't come out. Or . . . maybe they suffocated."

Nina stroked his arm. "Try not to think about it. I'm sure they're all right, you were just lucky to get out first. What happened next?"

"The tunnel. It ran in both directions, I think, but one way was blocked by soil and rocks. So I went the other way. I walked for a long time, and then the tunnel split into two. One of them sloped upward, so I chose that one. And then . . . then there was like a gust of air from below. And noise. At first I thought it must be rescue workers, so I headed back. I called out so they could find me. I shouted, 'It's me, it's Ivar.' And then."

Ivar had turned pale. He made several false starts before he spoke again. "And then someone answered. But something was off about it. The same words came back: 'It's me, it's Ivar.' At first I thought it was an echo, but then the words, the words changed places. 'Ivar me it's, me Ivar it's, me me me.' And then more voices joined in, until it was like a choir, shouting the same words over and over again: 'It's Ivar, it's Ivar.' It was like when children copy you, like when they do it to be mean."

He shuddered. "I didn't stop to see what it was. I just ran the other way. The tunnel kept branching off. I just picked whichever one, at random. But then I found a ladder, just like that. I ran straight into it and banged my shoulder. I climbed it, it was a very long ladder, but there was an opening at the top. I had to squeeze out. It was a pipe— I'd crawled out of a pipe. Then I saw Amatka's train station in the distance, straight ahead. I had ended up all the way out there. They found me when I reached the station. And then they examined me, and tomorrow I have to go in for a hearing." He slumped back in his chair, as if all the talking had spent the last of his remaining strength.

"A pipe," Vanja said.

Ivar sighed through his nose and closed his eyes. "They found me at the edge of town. They said I must have gotten confused and wandered out of the farm without anyone noticing."

"What?" Vanja said.

"If you were hallucinating, that could be indicative of brain injury," Nina said.

Ivar raised a hand. "I wasn't hallucinating. The tunnels are there. The pipes are there. I didn't wander out of the farm. I came from across the tundra."

"Could it be like at Essre?" Vanja asked. "I mean, like what I've heard anyway. The remains of people who lived here before us."

Nina frowned. "We don't know that. And I'm certain that I've never seen any pipes out on the tundra."

"Like you've been out on the tundra a lot?" Vanja asked. "What do you know that we don't?"

"Let's just leave it," Nina said. "Please."

Ivar got to his feet. "I need some sleep." He left his coat hanging on the back of the chair and went up to his room.

Nina remained at the table, her arms crossed. "What do you think—" Vanja began.

Nina interrupted her. "No. That's enough."

THIRDAY

Vanja woke up as Nina got out of bed and went downstairs. She could hear a stranger's voice in the hallway. More footsteps, and Ivar's voice on the landing. A short conversation. Footsteps. A door slamming shut. Then silence. When Vanja stuck her head out, the house was empty. She quickly got dressed and checked the time. She was late for work.

When Vanja arrived at the office, Anders was already stamping the forms that had been delivered that morning. He took a step back, smiled, and handed her the rest of the stack.

"You're thirty-two minutes late," he said. "How is your house-mate?"

"He's back," Vanja replied. "He's all right."

"Great," Anders said. "He's upstairs."

"Here?"

"For the interview."

Vanja stamped the rest of the forms, all the while glancing furtively at the corridor.

About an hour later, Ivar came downstairs. He looked haggard. He greeted Vanja with a small wave. "Just fine," he replied when Vanja asked how he was feeling.

His voice was faint, as if he didn't really have the strength to speak. "It was an in-depth interview."

"Are you hungry? I've got my midday break soon."

Ivar shook his head. "No. I'm a bit tired."

Vanja lowered her voice. "What did you talk about?"

Ivar looked at the floor. "They took me to a room. They asked me what happened. I told them about how I fell into a small cavity underneath the mushroom farm, fainted, and was pulled out by the rescue workers. My housemates can confirm that I was a little confused last night. That I said some things I didn't mean." He looked back up at Vanja. "Right?"

Chills ran down Vanja's back. At the edge of her vision she could see that Anders had stopped leafing through the papers on his desk. "Of course," she said. "That's what Nina and I said to each other, that you must have had a little concussion or something."

Ivar nodded. "I'm going to the clinic now," he said. "I'm having another checkup."

He left. Vanja went back to sorting forms. She did it quickly, to keep her fingers from trembling. As soon as her midday break came, she walked over to the library.

Evgen was alone at his desk. He locked the door and got out his packed lunch while Vanja told him everything: how Ivar had disappeared, wandered through the tunnels, gone in for an "interview," and come back with a different story. Evgen ate with his eyes fixed on Vanja, his fork moving mechanically between his lunch box and his mouth.

When Vanja finally fell silent, he put the fork down and swallowed. "They've probably filled the hole in already."

"But do you agree with Ivar, that the tunnels were there already?" Vanja asked.

"Let's see what the library says," Evgen replied.

He got up and walked over to one of the bookcases. He crouched in front of a shelf near the floor and ran his fingers along the spines, then pulled out a book: *About Amatka's Geography*.

Evgen opened the book to the first page. "Layout of the colony, structures, installations. Mushroom farm." He leafed through the book. " 'The mushroom farm is located at a depth of a hundred feet and covers an area the same size as Amatka. It was originally planned to be built in two levels; however, the bedrock below a hundred feet consists of a species of rock so hard that conventional excavation methods have failed. The advantage of this is, naturally, that Amatka rests on an extremely solid foundation.' "

He closed the book. "There you have it. In other words, either the tunnels were dug in secret—or someone else dug them."

"What do you believe?" Vanja asked.

"I believe anything's possible," Evgen replied. "And I believe the committee knows." He ran his tongue between his teeth and cheek. "So, a pipe out on the tundra. I've never seen that."

Nina met her at the front door of the house. "Ivar isn't feeling well."

"Did something else happen?"

Vanja looked over Nina's shoulder. Ivar sat by the kitchen table, his head bowed low. Ulla sat next to him with a hand on his shoulder.

"The hearing at the commune office, and then the same thing at the clinic. They really worked him over." Nina crossed the room to the kitchen cabinet and took out a plate for Vanja.

"I can't go back down there." Ivar's voice was weak and hollow. He muttered a muddled stream of words into his plate. "Nothing I've seen exists. They explained that to me. But I know. That they're there. The tunnels. And people, that there's people. The doctors say I had a concussion. Maybe the doctors and Nina are right. Maybe I've lost my mind. Because that's the truth, isn't it? That the tunnels don't exist? Because I'm the only one who saw them. And the voices. I've had a nervous breakdown. Everyone knows I have mental problems. They said as much, my 'mental health is fragile.' " He sniffled.

Nina sat down across from him and took one of his slender hands in hers. "Having a concussion isn't the same as being mentally ill, Ivar."

"I heard the doctors talking to one another. They talked about doing a procedure," Ivar told the plate. "I know what a procedure is."

"I know you do, dear," Ulla said and patted his shoulder.

Vanja glanced at Nina and hesitated. She knew how Nina would react, but she squared her shoulders and said it, for Ivar. "We could go there. I mean, back to where Ivar said he climbed out. Just go there and look, so he can see that he's not crazy. . . ."

Nina's lips narrowed. "That's really not a good idea."

"But if they're ruins, then it's the same as at Essre. Then they've always been there. Then it doesn't matter. Let's just take a look? For Ivar's sake. People are going there anyway. They have to investigate."

Nina shook her head. "Then that's what we'll let them do. We're not going to run off and do something stupid. Are we, Vanja?"

Vanja avoided her eyes. "No," she mumbled. "It was silly of me."

"I know what a procedure is," Ivar said loudly. "They drill into your head and stir your brains around."

Nina tried to soothe him. "No one's going to drill into your head, Ivar."

"Technically," Ulla said, "they don't actually stir your brains around. They sever the connections to the prefrontal cortex."

Ivar burst into tears.

Nina glared at Ulla. "Thanks for that."

"We all know there's a risk," Ulla said. "Even if you won't admit it. Even if these . . . ruins . . . have been here since before."

"Excuse me," Nina said, and went upstairs.

Ulla gave Vanja an amused grin. "I think we both know what's what," she said. "I think you should go look."

"Do you know something?" Vanja said.

"What are tunnels for?"

"What do you mean?"

"What does one use tunnels for?"

Vanja shook her head. "I don't understand."

"Travel," Ulla said. "One uses them to travel."

———

Later, when Vanja lay with Nina's arms around her, her breath in tickling gusts against the back of her head, it was hard to tell which was worse. That she'd lied to Nina when she'd promised her she wouldn't go out there. Or that Nina might be right, and that by going out there, Vanja would make things worse.

FOURDAY

It was still dark outside. The office wouldn't open for another couple of hours yet. Nina was fast asleep. Vanja stole out of bed and brought her clothes downstairs to the bathroom, where she got dressed. She didn't bother with food.

A few workers were out in the streets, pale and drawn from a long shift at work or too little sleep at home, staring blindly at the ground or out into space with bloodshot eyes. Following Ivar's description, Vanja walked straight west, past the station and across the railway tracks. After that, there was just the grass and the sky.

The grass rustled in the soft breeze. Vanja's boots splashed into little puddles that dotted the steppe, invisible in the gloom. She walked on until she came to the foot of a small rise. Something stuck out of the ground on the other side. It was too dark to make it out clearly. For a brief moment it was like standing on the hillock outside Essre, and she was sure of what she'd find on the other side: the silhouettes of asymmetrical buildings, little shapes moving between them. Then she reached the top and looked down the other side.

It wasn't just the one pipe but several, visible as dark shadows against the gray sky. Some were straight, some curved at a right angle at the top. A sudden cone of light hit one of the pipes, revealing a yellow surface with riveted joints. Its angled opening was torn, as if something had burst out of it with great force. The light moved on. Someone was walking around among the pipes. More figures joined the first, bringing more light. Vanja flattened herself against the ground. Cones of light swept across green protective suits. The shortest pipe ended at head height; some of the others were twice as tall. All of them looked easily wide enough to crawl into. The people in overalls didn't make any attempts, though. They took measurements, made notes, and talked among themselves. One of them opened up a canister and started to paint letters on the pipes. Two others began picking their way up the slope. Vanja crawled backward until she reached flat ground, then ran north at a crouch. If those people were going anywhere, it was probably back to Amatka. She looked back to see the beam of a flashlight sweeping across the rise. She lay down on her stomach again and waited. She hadn't run like that for a long time; it was hard to breathe without making noise. She pressed her mouth into the grass. The scent of wet vegetation and cold filled her nostrils. More silhouettes carrying flashlights arrived at the top of the rise. They were walking very slowly. One of the beams swung her way and then back again. The sky was growing lighter; they would be able spot her any moment now. She rose into a crouch and ran farther north.

If she hadn't banged her shin on its edge, she would have run right past the low pipe in the semidarkness. She toppled over and for a moment could do nothing but hold her leg and whimper. When the pain had subsided somewhat, she sat up and peered down. The opening was perhaps three feet across. On the inside, right below the edge, she could glimpse the rungs of a ladder. She leaned closer to the opening to listen. At first, there was only the pounding of her pulse in her ears, the wind rushing across the edge of the opening, the echo of her breathing. Then, something like distant music, a snatch of notes forever repeating. She listened for a long moment but couldn't decide if it really was music or her own head trying to create order from chaos.

It occurred to her that more rungs in the pipe had become visible. She looked up at the gray expanse of the sky, which was ever so slowly growing brighter. In the old world, the sky had been full of light. Lars had said so: that the sky was blue in the daytime and black at night, and that glowing lights traversed the sky, and one could follow their paths with one's eyes. That it was sometimes overcast, but that was only vapor; the sky was still there behind it. That there was something beyond the clouds, something that moved. This was always followed by Vanja's inevitable question: Is there something behind the gray of our sky?

We don't know, Lars had said. *Maybe, maybe not.*

The inhabitants of Colony Five had thought there was. They missed the skies of the old world. They longed for light. They talked about it so much that something finally appeared: a sun, a white-hot sphere that broke through the sky and burned the colony to a cinder. Such is the world in which we live, Teacher Jonas said. The words need guarding. A citizen who doesn't guard their words could destroy their commune.

Vanja arrived at the office just before eight. Today's first batch of forms was already on the reception desk, together with a handwritten note:

Anders is off sick today. Kindly tend to his tasks when you have completed your own. —Sec.

She took the note and walked upstairs to the long corridor of small offices on the first floor. The first office belonged to the head secretary, a graying woman in her fifties dressed in a rumpled green shirt. She was hunched over a ledger but looked up with a benevolent smile when Vanja opened the door. "Anders is off sick," Vanja said.

"Yes." The secretary nodded and continued to write in the ledger, with a dry, scratching noise.

"I don't know what Anders's tasks are."

The secretary firmly underlined something. "Oh. You haven't watched him work?"

Vanja considered this. "I suppose I haven't," she replied. "I've been very busy."

Moving with deliberate slowness, the secretary put her pen down and looked up at Vanja. There were dark circles under her eyes. She gave Vanja another smile. "Sort incoming reports, write a summary, file or dispose of reports as needed. There's a marking schedule on the notice board. And a manual under the reception desk."

"I see," Vanja replied. "I'll go do that, then."

The secretary nodded slowly. "Very good." She turned back to her ledger.

Vanja returned to the reception and looked for the manual. The space behind the desk was filled with carefully sorted rubber stamps, blank forms, notepads, sharpened pencils in a small cup, stackable letter trays.

She found the manual in a drawer under the desk: a small stapled bundle of good paper describing daily routines, marking order, emergency procedures, and instructions for machinery that Vanja didn't recognize and hadn't actually seen anywhere in the office. While she browsed through the manual, another courier arrived with more documents.

She started by separating forms from reports. The reports came in thin folders printed with titles like *Patient Statistics: Clinic Department 3*, or *Report: Results of the New Hygiene Protocol*, or *Follow-Up: Special Diet Plan for Mushroom Farmers with Dermatological Issues.* The receptionist's task was to record the total number of reports into a log along with titles, a summary of the contents, and date of registration; sign it; and then date the signature. After that, everything had to be filed according to a system that the manual needed three pages to describe. Vanja realized that Anders had actually been going easy on her.

One of the reports gave her pause. The title was short: *Incident Report*. Vanja opened the folder. The account of the collapse in the mushroom farm took up only a single page. They called it a solidity incident. Information was scant: the floor had collapsed and exposed a hitherto unknown cavity. Said cavity was now sealed. Three workers had perished. That was all, except for a short sentence at the bottom of the page: *further information restricted, committee-level clearance.*

In other words, no reports of what she had seen on the tundra, or what Ivar had seen under the mushroom farm, would cross her desk.

Vanja quickly put the report aside when the courier returned with a fresh stack of papers, this time from a children's house. She would have to speed up if she were to have any hope of finishing today.

It was only when she had sorted, stamped, and entered everything into the books and worked through almost the whole midday break that Vanja realized she couldn't find the keys to the archive. She went back upstairs to the secretary, who pulled out a drawer and removed a small key from a key ring.

"I'm making a note of your loan of this archive key," the secretary said. "The time is thirteen twenty-two. You will return the key thirty minutes from now, at the latest." She put the key in Vanja's hand.

"What if I need more time?"

The secretary smiled and shook her head. "I'm sure you won't."

According to the wall clock above the door, Vanja had seven minutes left of her allotted archive time. She had filed everything except the incident report, which according to the manual belonged in the Incidents section of the drawer labeled MUSHROOM FARM. The section was empty. She slipped the folder in behind the divider and skimmed the other sections. They bore labels like PLANNING, ACTIVITY, STAFF, CONSTRUCTION. Behind the CONSTRUCTION divider lay a fat folder from which a corner of a yellowed sheet of good paper stuck out. Six minutes left. Vanja pulled the folder out and carefully leafed through the documents. This was an old file, the paper yellow and brittle. The contents were sorted in chronological order—blueprints, diagrams, and calculations, none of which Vanja could decipher but which probably referred to the construction of the chambers. A report from the committee meeting that approved the construction plan made things a little clearer. It was dated the sixday of the third month, year fifteen, written by Oltas' Raisa One. It began with a long enumeration of the agenda: opening the meeting; nominating and approving the president, secretary, members responsible for checking the report; establishing the meeting's validity; and approving the agenda. Finally, at Item 8, a clue.

Member Harjas' Gustaf Three presented the results of the preliminary investigation into the possibilities of a mushroom farm. The idea was to construct a system of farming chambers that could double as a shelter in case of a catastrophe or incident. The chambers would be separated by heavy doors, allowing for isolation of any one area if needed. However, the construction plan had to be revised:

Harjas' Gustaf informed the meeting that the geoscientists have encountered an exceptionally hard type of rock at a hundred-foot depth. It has proven resistant to all tools and methods at our disposal. Ellars' Karin suggested making an exception and consider the use of large-scale architecture.

Architecture? The term didn't make sense here.

Ellars' Karin's proposal was voted down unanimously, citing the catastrophe in Colony 5 and subsequent legislation. The committee rules that the mushroom farm be constructed in one level only, and the area doubled to compensate for lost space.

Had Ellars' Karin wanted to talk the tunnels into existence? But they had decided not to. And yet, Ivar had fallen through the floor and found something underneath. Someone else had made the tunnels, that much was clear.

The sound of footsteps coming down the stairs made her stuff the files back into the drawer as quickly as she could. Just as the drawer slid shut, the secretary appeared in the doorway. She was much taller than she had looked sitting down; she almost had to hunch to fit through the door.

Vanja held out the key. "I just finished."

The secretary gave Vanja a gentle smile that somehow made her feel as though she'd been caught red-handed.

She went over to the library after work. Evgen was alone at his desk. He waved at her when she entered.

Vanja sat down at the table in the middle of the room. "Don't you ever have any other visitors?"

Evgen joined her at the table, sitting down where he could keep an eye on the door. "Two or three a day, maybe. Fewer all the time."

"I went outside this morning. I saw the pipes with my own eyes."

Evgen listened wide-eyed as Vanja retold the events of the previous night. "Listen," Vanja said, leaning closer. "One of them is a little out of the way. You can't see it until you're right on top of it. I don't think anyone's spotted it yet. We could go there."

"And have a proper look?"

Vanja nodded.

"Didn't Ivar say there was something down there, that he was scared of something?" Evgen said.

"He did. But I want to know. And so do you."

Evgen drummed his fingers on the table. "That's true." He slammed his palm down with a bang. "Let's do it."

The door to the library opened. Two older women in baggy overalls with blackened knees came inside; farmers, probably, from the plant houses.

Evgen stood up. "Come back tomorrow, and we'll see if the book has been returned."

"Thank you very much." Vanja turned around, almost collided with one of the farmers, mumbled an apology, and left.

The rhythmic noise came from the wall to Ivar's room. Next to her, Nina sat up in bed. It was still dark. Vanja felt dazed; her eyes ached. She couldn't have been asleep for more than a couple of hours.

"What is he doing?" Nina whispered.

In one fluid movement, Nina slid out of bed, stood up, and opened the door to their room. Vanja followed a little more slowly.

Nina crouched next to the bed with her hands on Ivar's knees. Ivar himself was naked among the sheets, leaning against the wall. He was painfully thin. "Get a blanket from our bed, Vanja," Nina said without turning.

When Vanja came back with the blanket, Nina had sat down next to Ivar. Vanja helped her wrap the blanket around him.

Nina cradled the back of Ivar's head in her hand. "He was banging his head against the wall."

"I'm sorry," Ivar said. "I didn't realize. That I was making noise."

"Should we take you to the clinic, Ivar?"

Ivar shook his head, as much as he could with Nina's hand holding it. "No. No, no need. I just need some rest. Maybe something to help me sleep."

"Are you sure?" Nina bent forward, forcing him to look her in the eye. "Are you absolutely sure? Look, I know you don't want to be a burden. But you're allowed to be a burden right now, Ivar. I need you to be. If things are this bad, we need to get you some help."

"It's all right. I promise. It's just a bit of anxiety. It's nothing I haven't been through before. It's not like I was trying to hurt myself or anything. It was just like"—Ivar waved his hand forlornly—"like swinging your legs from a chair, you know." He pulled the corners of his mouth up in an attempt to smile.

Nina sighed. "I'll get something to help you sleep. And then I'll sit with you. If you won't let me do that, I'll fetch someone from the clinic. Understood?"

Ivar nodded.

Nina walked past Vanja where she stood in the doorway. "I'm getting him a pill."

Vanja sat down on the edge of the bed and looked at Ivar out of the corner of her eye. When Nina's steps had receded sufficiently, she leaned closer. "Would it help if you knew that what you saw was real?"

"They say it wasn't real. But it felt real. But then again, I'm not well, you know." He leaned his head against the wall.

"I believe you," Vanja said.

Ivar slowly rolled his head from side to side.

Vanja got up when Nina came back with something in her hand. "Here. It'll calm you down."

Ivar swallowed the pill and lay down. "I don't want to go to the clinic," he mumbled. "They'll drill a hole in my head."

"No, they won't."

Nina tucked the blanket around him. She gently stroked his forehead with her thumb, over and over again, until he closed his eyes.

Vanja took a deep breath. "I've seen it."

Ivar opened his eyes again. Nina's head slowly turned to look at her. "I've seen it," Vanja repeated. "The pipe that Ivar climbed out of. It's really there."

"Before or after?" Nina said quietly.

"What?"

"Before or after. Did you see it before or after Ivar came out of it?"

"I . . . after."

Nina stared at her without speaking.

"Is it my fault?" Ivar's voice was thin. "Did I do it?"

"Shh. You did nothing." Nina went back to stroking his forehead.

"You don't know that," he muttered.

"Yes I do. Now be quiet. Breathe in. And out."

Nina turned her back to Vanja and bent over Ivar. The two of them formed a little unit of their own. Vanja left the room. She crawled into her own bed, hovering between sleep and wakefulness until it was once again time to go to work.

FIFDAY

According to the requisition copy Vanja received for filing purposes, the turn to donate good paper had come to the clinic's psychiatric ward. They were to copy all their medical journals onto mycopaper and send the good paper originals to the commune office. Children's House One and Two had been given the same task, along with Retirement Home Three and Four. The purpose of the requisition was given as "establishment material," whatever that was. Vanja sorted the requisition copies into the Resource Management section of the Economy drawer in the Administration row of cabinets.

The gently implacable secretary gave her no opportunity to search the archive today, either. Vanja barely had time to sort everything into the right drawer and section before the secretary stood in the doorway again.

"This is very stressful," Vanja ventured. "I need more time."

The secretary chortled. "It doesn't look that way from where I'm standing. You're doing just fine."

This time, her smile didn't quite reach her eyes.

There were three other visitors at the library. Vanja loitered by the biographies, but the others were taking their time. They were involved in a lively conversation about the nuances of Berols' Anna's plant-house poetry and kept dragging Evgen into it. His clipped replies only seemed to fuel the discussion. Evgen made eye contact with Vanja but didn't seem able to contrive an escape.

Finally, Vanja walked over to the desk. "I was wondering if you could help me find something in the letter collection."

"Certainly!" Evgen got up and elbowed past a visitor who was just about to ask another question.

"Tonight," Vanja whispered when they had made it in among the boxes.

Evgen pulled out a box, opened it, and showed Vanja the contents. "Where?"

Vanja rummaged through the letters. "Plant House Eight. Northwest. At one o'clock." She closed the box.

"I'm sorry I didn't have that particular letter," Evgen said loudly. "They might have something at the commune office."

"Thanks anyway." Vanja put her hat back on and left Evgen to deal with the poetry connoisseurs.

Slow shadows moved across the plant-house wall. The night growers were among the very few workers who were up at night, but it was bright enough in the plant houses that they couldn't see outside.

They arrived at the same time. Evgen handed Vanja a flashlight. She grabbed him by the coat sleeve and guided him out on the tundra. The plant-house glow gave them a little light to navigate by. Vanja traced a wide arc around the hollow where the pipes grew and where there might be people, but near enough that she wouldn't miss the spot where that one lone opening was located.

They walked for a long time. Evgen stumbled several times on the uneven ground before adopting a knee-high gait, carefully walking heel to toe. Lights winked in the direction of the hollow to the southwest. Ahead, the darkness was almost absolute. Now and then, Vanja briefly turned her flashlight on, scanning the ground for the opening. Each time, she looked over her shoulder, half expecting the lights from the people in the hollow to home in on them. Nothing happened. When the glow from the plant houses had nearly faded, and they had walked so far across the hard ground that Vanja began to doubt that she'd ever find the right spot, the beam of her flashlight revealed an angular shape. Evgen gasped. He walked a slow circle around the pipe, shining his light down the shaft.

"Are you sure this wasn't here before?" Vanja asked.

"Am I sure?" Evgen crouched and tapped the metal. "I've never been out this far in this direction." He looked at her over the rims of his glasses. "Are you with me?"

"Are you?"

"I'm with you. But I'm nearly shitting myself." He let out a thin laugh.

"Me, too." Vanja's own laugh came out as a shrill giggle.

Evgen climbed in first. Vanja stuck the flashlight between her teeth and followed him. The rungs looked dull in the light from their torches, and they were rugged to the touch; it was easy to find purchase. The sound of their feet against the ladder was almost deafening inside the shaft. Vanja had counted one hundred and fifty rungs when Evgen finally said, "Found the bottom."

Vanja carefully put one foot on the ground and turned around, catching the beam from Evgen's flashlight straight in the eyes. "Ow."

"Sorry." Evgen pointed it away from her. "Which direction do you think Ivar came from?"

They were standing in a vaulted tunnel with smooth walls, just big enough that they could stand upright side by side. Both directions were pitch-black.

Vanja wiped her chin with her sleeve. She had drooled around the flashlight. "Amatka is that way. He must have come from there, right?" She pointed to where the colony should be and started walking.

The tunnel smelled of cold earth and stale air. The walls absorbed the beams of their flashlights and the sound of their footsteps. After what felt like a long time, something in the distance reflected the light: a plain door with a handle. Vanja grasped the handle and cautiously pushed it down. The door opened inward with a low creak.

On the other side the darkness was virtually solid. Behind her, Evgen's breathing was rapid and shallow. Vanja realized she'd been holding her breath. "Can you see anything?" Evgen whispered.

Vanja shone her flashlight into the murk. A broad staircase led downward, rough-hewn steps covered in a layer of dust. Vanja descended, keeping her beam of light fixed on the steps.

Behind her, Evgen shone his flashlight upward. "I can't see the ceiling."

He was right, the ceiling was out of sight. It either absorbed the light completely or was beyond the reach of their feeble beams. The echo of their footfalls was faint and scattered. The air gradually became warmer.

Vanja halted. She should have noticed earlier. "There are no footprints."

Evgen stopped next to her. "There are no footprints on the stairs," she repeated. "Ivar said he climbed a staircase. But there's no trace of him here."

"Maybe he came from the other direction. Maybe we should have walked the other way when we came down the ladder."

"That doesn't make any sense. It leads away from Amatka."

"If you got the direction right, sure. And if the tunnel is completely straight."

Vanja clenched her teeth. "Just a little farther. We can always turn back."

The staircase ended in another door. When Vanja pushed the handle down, it opened outward with a groan. Judging from the echo, they were now standing in a very large space. Something was dripping in the darkness.

Vanja shone her flashlight on the floor. "How far did we walk, d'you think?"

"We could very well be underneath Amatka now," Evgen replied. "We would be under the mushroom farms, in that case. It smells . . . it smells like metal in here."

He made a small sound of surprise. The room grew darker. "Turn off your flashlight, Vanja."

"Why?"

"I want to try something. Turn off your flashlight."

Darkness rushed in. Vanja fumbled for Evgen, got hold of a corner of his coat, and hung on to it. A tug at her anorak told her he'd done the same. Then she realized that the darkness wasn't complete. A greenish glow emanated from the walls, brightening as they watched. Silhouettes emerged.

Beside her, Evgen let out a laugh. "Gleam lichen. I thought I saw something."

They were standing in a large chamber. In the middle of the floor sat a huge contraption, partly covered in the luminescent lichen. It looked at once both mechanical and organic, its details distinct from one another but with rounded edges and surfaces that seemed to have pores. Vanja could make out what looked like pistons, plungers, vents, an enormous cylinder. High above their heads, sheathed in the soft light, rose the arch of a spoked wheel whose highest point seemed to have merged with the ceiling.

"It's a machine." Saying it sent a chill down Vanja's spine.

Vanja and Evgen walked a full lap around it. Liquid bled from the ceiling and dripped onto it, settling in hard patches that choked the organism growing on the surface.

"Once when I was a boy, we went to Essre," Evgen said. "We visited the Pioneer Museum. They had a steam-powered machine there, a small one. Someone had brought it from the old world. It looked a bit like this." Evgen gestured at the wheel looming above them. "The wheel went round and round. Have you seen it?"

Vanja nodded. "Once. Then they removed it."

"Did Ivar say anything about a machine?"

"No," Vanja said. "I wonder if we went the wrong way. Or if it wasn't here before."

Evgen shone his flashlight at the walls. "I wonder if there are more exits."

Vanja took a mitten off and ran her hand over the machine's hull.

It gave off a slight vibration at her touch. "That little machine in Essre was supposed to power other machines. I wonder what this one is for."

"I don't like this place," Evgen said. "We should get out of here."

There was a circular plaque on the cylinder's hull. It reminded Vanja of a clock, but the symbols inscribed on the face looked unfamiliar. She tried to make out the symbols, but they kept drifting out of focus; she could almost read them, but not quite. If she could just concentrate for a moment.

"Vanja!" Evgen said it loudly, right behind her. She realized he'd called her name several times. "Can't you hear me?" His voice was thin. "I can't find the door."

Vanja straightened reluctantly. "What do you mean?"

"I mean I can't find the door."

His face appeared next to hers, eyes wide between the hat and his dewy beard. Vanja took her hand off the machine and turned on her flashlight. She aimed it at the wall but couldn't see anything at this distance. She glanced at Evgen, who looked back at her. They slowly walked over to the spot where the door should be. The wall was unbroken and black.

"Let's follow the wall," Vanja said. "We just missed it."

They followed the gentle curve of the wall. After a while, Vanja spotted tracks in the dust in front of them: two pairs of footprints, starting at the wall and leading to the center of the room. Another set of footprints returned from the center. No door. She stopped short. Next to her, Evgen grabbed her hand and squeezed it so hard it hurt. The pain cleared her head.

Vanja took a deep breath. "The door is here somewhere. We're just a little scared and confused." She squeezed Evgen's hand back. "Aren't we, Evgen?"

"Yes." Evgen's voice was barely more than a whisper.

Vanja spoke more loudly. "The door is exactly where we last saw it. The door is still there."

"The door is still there."

"Do you remember what it looks like?" Vanja said. "It opens into the chamber, I remember that."

"It's gray. And has a plain handle."

They continued around the room. The colossus in the middle of the chamber constituted a very insistent presence.

Evgen clutched Vanja's hand even tighter. "How many hinges does the door have?"

"Two hinges," Vanja said. "And it's a matte gray. Not shiny."

Further ahead, Vanja could see their footprints again, the ones leading toward the machine. And there, in the wall, where the footprints started: the door. She let out a long breath.

Evgen pushed the door open with a faint squeak. On the other side, the broad staircase rose up into the darkness. He rushed upstairs, two steps at a time. Vanja took one last look over her shoulder. It was as if the machine made a noise, a note so deep she could only feel it as a vibration in the pit of her stomach.

The steps felt much higher than when they had descended. Vanja's thigh muscles burned every time she heaved herself upward. It was with relief she saw the door at the top of the stairs—both because she'd reached the top and because the door was still there. Evgen leaned on the door and pushed it open. They jogged down the tunnel, Evgen's breath like tortured groans behind her.

Finally, a row of rungs broke the smooth wall. Vanja clambered up the ladder, almost slipping a few times. Cold, fresh air was blowing down the shaft. No light made it this far down, but she could hear the wind whistle across the opening. When she finally made it up, she heaved herself over the edge, fell down on the grass, and stayed there. Evgen collapsed on the ground next to her. They lay like that, staring up into the night sky, until they could breathe again. Eventually, Vanja stood up on unsteady legs. Evgen held out a hand, and she helped him up. Amatka's lights gleamed on the horizon. They started walking.

"It opened away from us," Vanja mumbled after a moment.

"What?" Evgen stopped.

"The door. When we came into the chamber with the machine. The door opened into the chamber."

Evgen nodded.

"But when we found it again," Vanja went on, "then it was turned the other way. It opened onto the stairs."

They stared at each other for a long moment. Evgen abruptly leaned over and vomited.

Nina was still fast asleep when Vanja stole into bed. It wasn't long until dawn. Then Ivar would get up, and she'd tell him that it was all true, that he wasn't insane. That there really was something underneath the colony.

The tunnels they had gone through—it was either a system or the tunnels themselves shifted. That, or Ivar had seen the machine but not mentioned it. Who had built the machine? Who had dug the tunnels? What were they for? *Travel,* Ulla had said. *Tunnels are for travel.* Who was traveling to Amatka? The memory of her dream by the lake came back: feet across the ice, voices, flutes. Voices had called out to Ivar underground. Amatka wasn't alone anymore.

SIXDAY

It was well after the breaking of the ice. Vanja had taken yesterday's leftovers out of the fridge and was reheating them on the stove. The coffee was brewing. She could smell Nina on her clothes.

The steps coming down the stairs were slow and heavy. Nina entered the kitchen with a small note in her hand. She sat down at the kitchen table in silence. Vanja took the pan from the heat and plucked the note from between Nina's fingers.

> *I know you don't believe it but they're going to come get me to do a procedure on me. I'm heading out on the ice. Don't tell the children what I did. They shouldn't have to hear it. I'm sorry.*

Nina scrunched her face up. She pressed her fists against her eyes. "I can't. I can't go down there."

Her body was so taut it trembled.

Vanja wrapped her arms around Nina from behind and put her cheek against hers. "I'll go."

The streets were almost empty in the gray light. It was far too early to be up on a Sixday. The only thing that moved was the shadow of the night growers on the plant-house walls. Vanja caught the sound of sprinklers as she passed, following the water-supply pipe to the lake. Stiff grass rattled against the irrigation pipeline. Vanja halted as an unfamiliar shape appeared at the edge of her vision. It stood far away on the tundra—long and thin, with a curved top end. Vanja squinted. It looked like a pipe, like the ones she had seen in a cluster the other night. Possibly. She turned in a slow circle and counted one, two, three slender silhouettes on the horizon, which until now had always been flat and featureless.

Vanja found Ivar's shoes among the rocks on the beach, and his coat at the water's edge. A ways out she could see the rounded shape of a back. Even though the waves seemed mere ripples on the surface, the body was drifting quickly toward the shore. Vanja took a couple of steps into the water, sucking in breath as her boots flooded with painful cold. She forced herself to move forward. After only a few feet, the water reached halfway up her thighs. She gasped as the cold made her legs burn, but the body was close enough now that she could grasp the pale yellow sweater. She pulled it to her and grabbed hold under the armpits. Only once the body was halfway out of the water did she turn it over.

Ivar had walked out on the ice dressed in nothing but his under-clothes, and the lake had thawed underneath him, dropping him into the frigid water. The warm tone of his skin had turned pallid. His eyes were only closed halfway, revealing a glimpse of dark brown iris. Vanja crouched next to him. She took her mitten off and gently stroked his cheek. It was cold and unyielding. His unrelenting frown had been smoothed out; his lips had parted slightly, as if in sleep. But Ivar himself wasn't in there anymore. Vanja carefully pulled him all the way out of the water. Thin as he was, his body was very heavy. She fetched his coat and draped it over him. It wasn't long enough to cover both his head and feet, so she chose the feet. Cold feet were the worst. "I went and looked." She tucked the edges of the coat under him. "I was going to tell you this morning. That you're not crazy, that there's something down there."

Talking made her throat ache. "I wish you could have waited just a little while." She patted his cheek. "I'm going to get some help. You won't have to stay out here."

Vanja walked back toward Amatka on numb legs. When she was almost there, she realized Ivar wasn't wearing a hat or gloves. He would be cold.

No. He wouldn't be.

At the clinic, two orderlies ushered her into an exam room, where they undressed her and swaddled her in heating blankets. They didn't seem surprised by what she'd found in the lake. "Here we go again," one of them said. "We'll send someone to get him."

"I have to tell our housemates," Vanja said.

They noted her address. Vanja wasn't allowed to go anywhere until they were sure she was unharmed.

They finally released her three hours later. Nina was still sitting at the kitchen table. She had stopped crying.

She looked up at Vanja, her eyes remote. "They were here."

"I had to stay at the clinic. The water, I went into the water to get him, it was cold."

Nina nodded. They were silent for a moment, Vanja by the door, Nina at the table. Finally, Nina pushed her chair back. Her voice was raspy and flat.

"Well, he finally went and did it. At least now I don't have to wonder when it's going to happen. That idiot. I saw it coming for years." She went over to the stove and started making coffee.

Vanja sat down and watched Nina do the dishes and then violently clean the counter and stovetop. Nina talked while she cleaned. She talked about a quiet boy who became a melancholy but kind youth, who became the Ivar of recent years, slowly wasting away. "They tried everything," she said. "Medication, light therapy, psychotherapy. Shocks. And at best he was . . . he functioned. He could get out of bed, get dressed, eat. He could go to work."

She had given up on drying her cheeks. Fresh tears ran down her face now and then, and dripped onto her sweater. "Maybe he would have been all right in the end. But then this. Or . . . maybe he would never have been okay. Maybe he was incurable. Maybe he was just broken." Her last word was accompanied by the loud bang of the scrubbed frying pan being slammed down on the counter.

Vanja topped up their cups. "I'm hungry," Nina said.

She walked over to the fridge and took out a bowl, then fetched a fork.

Vanja rose halfway from the chair. "Let me heat that for you."

"No need." Nina mechanically shoveled bits of mushrooms and root vegetables into her mouth. "Talk. Talk about something. Tell me about Essre."

Vanja told her about Essre: the square plant houses radiating out from the center; the massive commune office that housed the central administration; the circular streets; the throng of people. Nina stared into the wall, chewing and swallowing. When the bowl was empty, she pushed it aside.

"I know you're up to something," she said. "With the librarian, that Evgen guy."

Before Vanja had time to reply, Nina continued: "Are you fucking him?"

Vanja started. "What? No."

"Fine. Then what are you doing?"

"We talk."

"About what?"

Vanja turned to the window. "For example . . . what happened to Ivar. What's under the mushroom farm." She took a deep breath. "I went out last night. I went down that pipe. To prove Ivar right. I was going to tell him this morning. But when I woke up he was already gone."

Vanja braced herself and waited. When the silence went on unbroken, she glanced back at Nina, who had leaned back in her chair and sort of deflated. The shadows under her eyes were a bluish black. The rage had drained from her face, to be replaced by something worse. When she spoke, her words were almost inaudible. "You don't know what you're doing."

"I'm trying to help. To find the truth. To make things better. Down there, there's . . ."

Nina held up a hand. "No. What you don't understand is that it only takes this much"—she pinched her thumb and forefinger together—"to destroy us all. And if things have already started happening, then you're making it worse."

"But how do you know? How can any of us know? How do we know it's bad? Maybe it's just different. Better. Nina, anything is better than this."

Nina gave her a look that made Vanja shrink back. "No. Anything is not better than this. I've seen Berols' Anna's colony. I know what happens."

Vanja was dumbfounded. "How? When?"

"No. No, enough of this." Nina held up both hands. "Just . . . leave it alone."

She got up from the table and went upstairs. Vanja heard one door bang shut, then another.

Vanja stood outside Nina's door for a long time, listening. At length she managed to muster enough courage to knock. No reply. She knocked again.

Eventually Nina opened the door. "What?"

Vanja's mind abruptly went blank. "I just thought, I don't know. I'm sorry." She couldn't think of anything else to say.

Nina breathed in through her nose. Her words were slow and her voice flat. "You can't help me right now. I want to be alone. You'd better leave." She closed the door again.

Vanja lingered for a moment, staring at the door. Of course.

There was nothing she could do. Nina and Ivar had been so close for so long, like brother and sister. What they had was so much bigger and more profound than what Vanja had with Nina. Anything Vanja did to comfort her would just be clumsy and clueless. At least today. She turned around and went back downstairs. Maybe Nina would want to be with her when she came back out. Or maybe not. She would grieve for a long time.

SEVENDAY

The leisure center filled up early. Instead of the usual games and organized play, a note by the entrance informed the crowd that song and poetry were on the program. The evening meal would be accompanied by a reading of Ivnas' Öydis's great poem "The Pioneers." After that, communal singing. And after that, more readings—excerpts from Berols' Anna's Plant House series and several other poems Vanja didn't recognize. It was remarkable that her poems were still allowed, considering what she did. Perhaps the power of her realist poetry was so strong that it outweighed her later deeds. And to the public she never did those other things, anyway. She had just died in the fire.

Vanja registered at the entrance, hung her anorak on a peg by the door, and looked around for a seat. The tables along the walls were almost full. Children who couldn't sit still were chasing each other below the dais at the far end of the hall. Only on Sevenday were they allowed to run wild like that. Vanja found a free seat at the end of a table. She greeted the others, who nodded, smiled, and returned to their conversations. Their murmur enveloped her.

Sometime later, the cooks emerged from the kitchen carrying huge pots to rapturous applause. Vanja's hands clapped along. Someone put a bowl in front of her. The clatter and banging of cutlery on bowl rims filled the air. After a while, Vanja became aware that someone had gently nudged her aside and now sat in her spot at the end of the table. It was Evgen. He had said something.

Vanja blinked. "What did you say?"

"I said hello." His face looked sallow.

"Hello."

"You look like I feel."

"Ivar killed himself," Vanja said.

Evgen's eyebrows shot up, but then he merely nodded. "Was he afraid they'd do a procedure on him?"

"How did you know?"

He smiled thinly. "It was a guess. It wouldn't be the first time."

They ate in silence for a while. The meal was a slapdash, over-salted stew of shiny mushroom caps. Further down the table, people had started drinking and were talking loudly. "I can't stop thinking about it," Evgen mumbled next to her.

"What's that?" Vanja put a spoonful of stew in her mouth and focused on chewing. The mushrooms were leathery and seemed to grow in her mouth as she chewed.

"I can't stop thinking that the door might have led somewhere else, and that we're not in the real Amatka anymore." He hacked at an agaric with his fork. "I know it makes no sense, that can't be the case. I'm not saying I want it to be true. I just can't stop thinking about it." He pinched the bridge of his nose between his thumb and forefinger. "Because this fake Amatka might be even worse than my own."

Vanja glanced out at the crowded hall. "You probably shouldn't say things like that in here."

"If we're in fake Amatka, maybe the rules don't apply." Evgen giggled.

One of their neighbors shot them a glance. Vanja managed a hollow laugh and elbowed Evgen in the ribs. "You're impossible!"

Evgen laughed back. "You bet!"

Their neighbor turned his attention back to his own company. A tapping noise from the podium made them fall silent. It was time for the first reading of the night.

When they had sung "The Pioneer Song," their host called the children up on the dais.

"And now it's fun time for the children!" he shouted. "We're going to sing 'The Marking Song'!"

They sang several rounds of "The Marking Song." The children took turns pointing to different objects in the room, and everyone laughed whenever it was tricky to fit the words in. After six rounds, it was time for "The Farmer Song," and after that "When I Grow Up." There was a quiz, too. Extra credits were awarded to citizens who answered questions about the number of houses in the colony and the number of inhabitants and streets correctly. Even more credits went to comrades who could name all the different types of buildings, their functions, and the number and names of the mushrooms grown in the chambers. Then they all sang "The Marking Song" again.

On the dais, their host's gestures grew ever wilder and more sweeping, until he finally gave up his spot for a poetry recital. While the reader slowly chanted his way through "The Streets," the host took a seat in a corner by the coatroom. The happy grin had vanished from his face. He looked sweaty and feverish. He'd found a bottle of liquor somewhere and was swigging straight from it. When he noticed Vanja watching him, he bared his teeth in a grimace and waved at her. It took her a moment to realize it was supposed to be a smile. She waved back.

Ulla was in the kitchen, putting on her boots. She looked up at Vanja with a small smile. "Going somewhere?" Vanja asked.

"Just out for an evening stroll," Ulla replied. "Did you notice the pipes? No one else seems to have."

Vanja paused. "I had forgotten about them somehow. What with Ivar . . ."

"Of course."

"Ulla, what's going on?"

Ulla finished tying her boots. "What do you think?"

"I think you know exactly what's happening," Vanja said.

Ulla stood up. She seemed younger somehow, more sprightly. "You want freedom," she said. "Don't you?"

"I do," Vanja whispered.

"So do I," Ulla replied. She squeezed Vanja's arm gently. "Go to bed."

Nina had fallen asleep in Ivar's bed with her face buried in his pillow. She was wearing one of his sweaters. Vanja went into her own room. She hadn't been in there for days except to sleep and fetch new clothes. She took a turn around the room, touching furniture and objects. Then she curled up on the bed with her clothes on.

THE FOURTH WEEK

FIRSTDAY

When the thunder of breaking ice died down, it was as though it left a buzz in the air. Not quite audible, it was more a sensation than a sound. Nina was still in Ivar's bed. When Vanja sat down on the edge of the bed, Nina turned her face to the wall and pulled the blanket over her head. Vanja went down to the kitchen. It was chilly, somehow bigger and emptier than before. She made coffee and porridge, too much porridge—since Ivar wasn't going to have any. She filled two bowls and left the rest on the counter to cool.

Nina didn't react when Vanja put a bowl and a cup of coffee down on her desk. Vanja ate her own porridge in the kitchen, washed the dishes, and sat back down at the table. The silence was compact, except for that low drone she couldn't quite hear. Eventually it was time to put the leftovers in the fridge and go to work.

A janitor arrived midmorning, carrying a bucket and a stack of good paper. She greeted Vanja curtly and came in behind the counter uninvited. Then she picked a paintbrush out of the bucket and slathered some of its contents on the wall. She dropped the brush back into the bucket, leafed through the papers, and slapped one of them in the middle of the sticky mess on the wall. She walked around the counter to the front of the reception, repeated the procedure, and left without another word.

THIS NOTE DESCRIBES:
THE COMMUNE OFFICE RECEPTION AND ARCHIVE

The reception occupies a total area of 366 square feet. The space is furnished with one (1) reception counter with drawers, two (2) writing desks, six (6) storage shelves, and three (3) office chairs. The storage shelves contain assorted office supplies (see separate list of contents), two (2) typewriters, one (1) duplicating machine, and manuals, log books etc. (see separate list of contents). The staircase to the reception archive is furnished with doors at both ends and has eighteen (18) steps of standard height. The archive contains twenty (20) filing cabinets with drawers containing archive material (see separate list of contents). From the archive, one (1) security door leads to the Secure Archive (see separate list of contents).

The paper had been hastily de-inked and reprinted. Here and there, Vanja could make out the faint remains of words that had previously filled the page: "beloved," "waiting," "mine." A love poem. Vanja walked around the counter to inspect the other note. Part of a verse from a nursery rhyme was vaguely visible between the new letters. These were pages from the confiscated library books. This was apparently one of the things the committee needed all the good paper for: description.

Brisk steps approached from the stairs that led to the offices. A courier in gray overalls and tightly braided hair shot around the corner and snapped to attention in front of Vanja.

"Good morning!" she blurted. "I am here to announce that the committee has instituted an additional leisure night! Every Thirday night at eighteen o'clock all citizens will attend their respective leisure center to partake in delightful games, quizzes, and group conversations! Hooray for Amatka's commune!"

"Hooray!" Vanja replied.

The courier turned on her heel and marched into the colony streets. In her wake, a swarm of vigorous boys and girls in identical overalls trooped down the hallway toward the exit.

Vanja fingered the note on the wall. Those kids probably had no idea why there were suddenly two leisure nights a week. But the committee must have known for some time.

Nina was sitting up in bed when Vanja went to check on her. The porridge bowl was still full, but the coffee cup was empty. When she spoke, she sounded lucid but monotonous, her eyes fixed on something in the far distance. Someone from the clinic had been there to check why Nina hadn't shown up for work. She had been given a week's leave for personal reasons.

"I have to go see Ivar," she said. "They only keep bodies for forty-eight hours before recycling." Her eyes focused on Vanja for the first time. "Could you come with me? Right now?"

"Of course." Vanja picked up the sweater and trousers Nina had dropped on the floor sometime during the night or day. "Shirt, trousers. You need to eat something first."

Nina got dressed, followed Vanja into the kitchen, and mechanically ate the reheated porridge Vanja put in front of her. When she'd managed half of it, she got to her feet. "Let's go." She put her jacket on without buttoning it and walked outside with long strides.

Ivar lay on a gurney. They'd wrapped him in a white shroud, leaving only his head uncovered. Nina sat down on a stool next to the gurney and just looked at him. Vanja stayed in the doorway. Britta had once told her there was nothing scary about dead people; they just looked like they were sleeping. When Vanja had pulled Ivar out of the water, she could still tell it was Ivar, but he hadn't looked like he was sleeping. He had looked like he was dead. Ivar without Ivar inside. The thing on the gurney wasn't even Ivar, just an object that resembled him a little.

Nina let out a shaky sigh and caressed the corpse's cheek. "What am I going to tell the girls, Ivar? What am I supposed to say?"

When the names of the recently deceased were recited next Sevenday, Ivar's name wouldn't be among them. No one would observe a minute's silence for him. Taking a life, one's own or someone else's, was the most disloyal action of all; every lost life put the colony's survival in peril. Murderers were no longer citizens. Ivar would be sent to recycling, and then he'd be gone, erased.

"Tell them what happened," Vanja said from the doorway. "They deserve to know."

"Do you think they want to carry that around? That their father was a suicide?"

Vanja took a few steps closer. "No," she said quietly. "It wasn't Ivar, not really. You know whose fault it was."

Nina rested her head on the edge of the gurney. "You win. I'll tell you everything."

It was Distillate x 2 this time, a little stronger. They sat in Ivar's room with the door closed, curled up on his bed. Nina still hadn't let Vanja touch her. She downed a whole cup before speaking.

"I'm telling you all this so you'll understand," Nina said. "We will never speak of this again."

Vanja nodded.

"And after I'm done," Nina continued, "there will be no questions, no discussions, nothing. Understood?"

"Understood."

Nina poured herself more liquor. "I was nineteen. I'd just received my nursing diploma. A hundred people disappeared overnight. Poof, gone. Someone had left a manifesto at the commune office, signed by Berols' Anna. I remember she'd just finished her Plant House series. She won an award for it. So, somehow she managed to organize all these people without anyone knowing. I had no idea what was going on. No one I knew had any idea. But everyone knew someone who had disappeared."

"What did the manifesto say?"

"Don't know the details. It was never made public. Those of us who went on the expedition were told a little, just enough to make sure we'd be prepared. It said something along the lines of they were going to found a new colony, and that it would be more real somehow. That they'd do it right. But people in Amatka didn't know about the manifesto. At first, all we knew was that people had disappeared, but not why. People panicked. There were all sorts of rumors, like about a suicide pact or some kind of abduction. Then, after a few days, I was called up to join the expedition. That's when I found out. The committee had decided we couldn't afford to lose that many citizens, so even if they were disloyal, they had to be brought back home."

Nina stared into space for a moment. "It took us a while to find them." She took a swig from her cup. "We bumped about in a terrain vehicle for days. And, you know, no one had ever been that far from Amatka. We were so scared something would happen to us. We drove around the lake. There was nothing out there, just water on one side and tundra on the other, but it was still terrifying. Because it didn't end, you know. It just went on and on." Nina gesticulated with her free hand. "Completely featureless as far as the eye could see." She topped up her cup again and drank half of it down, shuddered, then patted her chest. "And then we saw it. It was like a hole in the sky. It grew bigger as we drew near. And when we arrived . . . I thought it was, I don't know what it was. We'd come to a halt, but we just sat in there, staring like little kids. Then someone said: There are houses there. And there were, right under the hole. It looked sort of like a colony—a ring of little houses and a commune office. We put our protective suits on, the supersafe kind with visors and everything, and we stepped out of the vehicle. It was like, like a bubble. No, not a bubble. But the sky was different there, right above the houses. There were lights in the sky. I have to go to the toilet."

Nina abruptly got up and went downstairs. When she came back, her face was flushed and her breath sour. She waved Vanja's concern away and refilled her cup. "Okay, so we'd left the vehicle, and the expedition leader went first. She walked right up to the edge of the town. The rest of us were standing there, looking in."

"You said it looked sort of like a colony?"

Nina shook her head. "They'd painted murals on the walls. No words, no markings. But paintings of things that don't exist. Everywhere."

"But the people?"

Nina was quiet for a moment. "The things we saw in there weren't people. She, Berols' Anna, she came up to us. That's what it called itself, anyway. It, she, walked up to that wall. She didn't come over to our side, but we could hear her fine."

"But why would you say they weren't people?"

"Because . . ." Nina shook her head again. "They didn't look human anymore. They looked . . . sort of human? But not quite. Something about the way they moved, the way they looked at us. Like we were children." She took a deep breath. "Berols' Anna, when she spoke . . . her voice filled your head. She said three things. She said to leave them alone. And then she said . . ." Nina frowned.

Vanja waited.

" 'We've given ourselves over to the world,' " Nina said. "That's what she said, word for word. And then the third thing: 'We'll come to your aid soon.' "

"What did you do next?" Vanja asked.

"What could we do? No one wanted to head inside. We returned home. The committee swore us to secrecy. Anyone who talked about what happened would be taken care of and sent away. The committee was afraid that if others got wind of what happened, they'd try the same thing, they'd try to break out. Or that talking about what happened would spread Anna's ideas. It would destabilize the colony. So when we came home, someone torched a leisure center, and they made the official story that the missing people had died in the fire."

Nina cleared her throat. "I'm only telling you this so you'll get it.

Is this what you want, Vanja? You want things to be like Berols' Anna made them?"

"But maybe they're doing well in there," Vanja mumbled.

"They're not human anymore. You want to stop being human, is that it?"

Vanja looked away. She had an impulse to say yes but stopped herself and instead shook her head.

Nina emptied her cup. "So, that's that. And since that happened, it's been harder to maintain order—just look at the lake. Maybe it's because there are fewer of us. Or because what Berols' Anna did changed something. I don't know. But we can't afford to be lax like people in Essre apparently are. Of course, there are those who slack off. Fifteen years is enough for people to start to forget. And the children aren't told about this. They have to believe there was a fire."

She filled her cup again. Her speech had taken on the overly precise enunciation of the very drunk. "Maybe Ivar would still have been here."

"What?"

"Maybe Ivar would still have been here. If people had just followed the rules, then nothing would have fallen apart. Maybe that chamber wouldn't have collapsed."

Nina sniffled and wiped her cheeks with her palm. Then she fixed Vanja with bloodshot eyes. "I don't want to, because I care about you. But I'll report you if I have to. Promise me I won't have to."

"I promise," Vanja said.

Nina rested her head on Vanja's shoulder. Before long, her breathing grew more even and deepened. Vanja caught her cup the moment before it tumbled from Nina's hand.

She lay awake for a long time with Nina's arms wrapped around her. Ivar's gray face haunted her. Nina couldn't be right. Ivar was in pain because the committee forced him underground, because they wouldn't let him live his life the way he wanted. Not because of what he saw when the tunnel caved in.

When she finally drifted off, she found herself in the cave with the machine. The luminescent lichen festooned the surfaces in white and green. Everything was very still. The dripping noise had stopped. Then the engine shuddered to life with a screeching groan. The wheel tore free of the stalactites with a crash and slowly began to turn. Lichen and minerals scattered in a cloud.

She couldn't see what the machine powered.

SECONDAY

Anders was back. He stood behind the counter, blowing his nose into a soiled handkerchief. In front of him sat a stack of papers and folders.

"You're on time," he said when Vanja entered. "Good. The research division has given us work to do." He pushed the stack toward her. "These are requisitions and permission applications. We need them in triplicate, one copy for the archive and two for the office upstairs. They need to be processed and sent back to the research division immediately. So get going." He looked oddly exhilarated.

Anders sat down in front of his typewriter and hammered out what looked like reports. Vanja fetched blank forms and copying paper. She spent the morning translating the short messages in the stack on her right into applications. The research division was applying for equipment and workers. Their purpose wasn't stated very clearly; they made several references to some decision that the committee had reached the day before. It had something to do with object diagnostics and emergency protocols.

By the time she had finished typing up the forms, it was already time for the midday meal. Vanja delivered the copies to the secretary upstairs and then went straight to the canteen. Today's dish was bean stew. The atmosphere in the canteen was oddly subdued. People spoke in short, indirect bursts:

"Did you hear . . . ?"

"Yes. I got a summons. Hedda, too."

"One wonders what's going on."

"It's probably nothing."

"You're right, it's probably nothing."

The last sentence recurred in all conversations, repeated by everyone within earshot.

In the early afternoon, a band of couriers came downstairs and filed past the reception. One of them stopped at the desk; it was the same girl with braids who had been there the day before. She waved at Vanja and Anders to get their attention, held up a note, and recited: "INCREASED MARKING. In a campaign to improve the commune's well-being, normal activity will be suspended between fifteen and sixteen o'clock for marking of all objects in the area. This will be repeated every day until further notice. Hooray for Amatka's commune!"

"Hooray!" Anders hollered.

"Hooray," Vanja echoed.

Ivar's death certificate was delivered. Date of birth, date of death. He was thirty-two years old. Cause of death: self-inflicted hypothermia and drowning. As Vanja stood in the archive holding Ivar's file, she realized how easy it would be to just stuff the papers down her shirt or into the box of forms she'd brought downstairs. Nina could have some evidence of Ivar's existence to keep. The children would be able to remember their father. She pulled the papers out and began folding them so they'd take up less space. "Anything exciting?" Anders was standing right behind her, much too close, eyebrows raised.

Vanja stiffened and waved the papers around. "Nah."

"They're going to be scrapped, I take it. Given that you're not filing them." He took the papers out of her hand. "I'll do it for you, it's no bother." He tucked the thin stack under his arm and gestured at the door with his free hand. "Marking time!"

Anders tasked Vanja with marking office supplies in the small supply alcove. Every pen, paper clip, measuring stick, folder, envelope, and piece of paper might need to be named and re-marked. She started with the envelopes and went on to notebooks and paper. When she finished, it was already four o'clock. She would have to hurry if she hoped to get through the rest of the supplies in time. Behind her, Anders went downstairs to mark temporary folders.

Vanja emptied a box of pencils, lined them up on the shelf, and pointed at them one by one. "Pencil, pencil, pencil."

It wasn't long before the words flowed together. "Pencil-pencil-pencil-pen-cilpen-cilpen-cilpen-cilpen-cilpen—"

The last pencil in the row shuddered. As Vanja bent closer to look, the shiny yellow surface whitened and buckled. Then, suddenly and soundlessly, it collapsed into a pencil-shaped strip of gloop. Vanja instinctively shrank back. Her stomach turned. She had done it. She had said the wrong name, and the pencil had lost its shape. It shouldn't have happened that quickly. She extended a finger and let it hover just above the surface of the transparent sludge. Then she slowly lowered it.

The substance was tepid, warm almost, and made her finger tingle. It was slightly springy to the touch. It felt much like touching a mucous membrane, as though life surged just beneath the surface. When she removed her finger, the surface kept an imprint of her fingertip for a few seconds before springing back up. This was the one thing everyone feared. But it didn't feel dangerous. She touched it again. She'd always imagined that it must be cold and slimy, but the surface felt just like skin. Like a living creature.

Anders's footsteps could be heard coming up the stairs. He was singing an old love song, a waltz they'd played in the leisure center last Sevenday: "Pia, my pioneer, please say you hold me dear, say that you'll let me adooore youuu . . ."

"Pencil," Vanja hissed at the gloop. "Pencil. Pencil. Pencil."

Nothing happened. "Pencil," Vanja whispered in desperation. With a faint snapping noise, the gloop contracted into an oblong shape. It almost looked like a pencil. The surface had cooled, but was still soft. "Pencil." The material hardened slightly.

". . . tralala, no other giiirl for meee!" Anders exclaimed, and slammed the archive door shut. "How's it coming?"

"Just fine." Vanja closed her hand around the unfinished pencil and continued marking office supplies with her back to him.

"Good. This is important work we're doing! Important!" He patted Vanja's shoulder so hard it hurt.

At ten minutes to five, Vanja's throat was dry and her tongue felt stiff. "I'm done," she told Anders. "I can leave, right?"

Anders threw a thin stack of forms onto the counter next to her. "You need to file these."

They were forms Vanja had copied to fresh mycopaper earlier that morning.

"Go ahead," Anders urged.

Vanja swallowed her annoyance and went down to the archive. Anders remained at the counter, stamping something with those hard little thuds of his. Vanja pulled out drawers, filing papers at top speed so she would finally be allowed to leave. Her gaze fell on the secure archive. She'd only be given access with a commission of some sort. Or if she got hold of a key. Vanja fingered the object in her pocket. Or if she made a key. Before she could follow her train of thought, Anders called down the stairs that it was five o'clock.

Evgen sidled up next to her as she exited the building. "Is there somewhere we can talk? We can't go to the library."

"Why not?"

"We'll discuss it later. Is there somewhere? Your place?"

Vanja shook her head. Evgen pulled his hat further down his forehead and let out something between a whimper and a sigh. "What's going on with you?" Vanja asked.

"Meet me by Plant House Seven. Don't take the same route as me." Evgen turned south.

Vanja walked west, curving slowly toward the southwest and Plant House Seven. The plant houses began to glow in the gathering darkness as the growers inside switched their lamps on. The cold deepened noticeably with the fading light. At first, Vanja couldn't find Evgen anywhere. Then he stuck his head out from behind a stack of manure barrels at the far end of the plant house. In the nook between the barrels and the opaque gable wall, they were almost completely hidden from sight from all angles. Vanja huddled close to Evgen, who took his gloves off, wrung them, and put them on again.

"Listen," Vanja said before Evgen spoke. "I can confirm the whole story about Berols' Anna."

Evgen blinked. "How? Where? In the archives?"

"No. Nina. She was part of the rescue team."

Vanja recounted all she could remember of Nina's story. Evgen listened, all the while gazing out toward the horizon and fiddling with his gloves. When Vanja fell silent, he didn't speak at first. Finally, he nodded to himself.

" 'We will come to your aid soon,' was that it?"

"Yes." Vanja rubbed her mittens together. "What if they're already here?"

Evgen hummed. "My thought exactly."

"The tunnels. Ivar heard voices under the farm."

"You're thinking that they made the tunnels."

"That, or they've used them to travel here."

"And there's the machine."

Vanja shuddered at the thought. "Any thoughts on what it does?"

"No," Evgen said.

"I dreamed that it started moving."

"One should go down there to check," Evgen said.

"There's no way I'm going down there again," Vanja said. "I can't believe we did it last time."

"You're right," Evgen said. "They're probably there."

"But why is this happening now?"

"Maybe they couldn't do it before. Maybe it's become easier. Because there are fewer of us, or because more people are thinking along the same lines as you and I. We can't be the only ones."

"It *is* easier now." Vanja pulled her mitten off and took the pencil-thing out of her pocket.

Evgen leaned forward and squinted at it. "I dissolved it. And put it back together," Vanja said.

"Really?" Evgen's hand hovered over the pencil. Then he withdrew.

"Really."

"It's all happening at once." Evgen rubbed his forehead. "I brought you here to tell you that the papers are gone."

"What papers?"

"What papers? What do you think? In old Amatka. Someone took them."

"Are you sure?"

"What do you mean, am I sure!" Evgen's whisper went up an octave. He took a deep breath. "Of course I'm sure. I've kept them in exactly the same spot since I started collecting them. And now they're not there anymore, so someone must have taken them. Please tell me it was you."

"No. I haven't been back since the time you took me there."

Evgen breathed out through his nose in one short snort. Beads of moisture had formed on Vanja's eyelashes. Annoyed, she wiped them away and broke the silence. "What are you going to do?"

Evgen let out a shrill giggle. "It's just a matter of time. Either they know who I am, and they followed me there. Or they'll figure it out. Not a lot of people have access to those kinds of documents. It's over, Vanja." He pulled his coat tighter around him. "I'm going to be arrested. They'll probably do a procedure on me, too. Do you know what they do with people after? They dump them in a secret camp and leave them to die."

"I've seen it," Vanja said.

Evgen seemed not to hear her. When she met his gaze, his eyes were blank and feverish. "The question is what I can do before they take me in. We have to act before . . . Look, it's time. We have to do something, tonight. I have a plan. Follow me." He held out his hand.

"What's the plan, Evgen?"

"You won't like it," he said. "But if someone's down there, I think we should talk to them."

Vanja froze. "No," she said.

"They're coming to help us," Evgen said. "Remember?"

"Evgen, wait," Vanja said. "I have to go home to Nina, she needs me. And if I don't come home . . . she'll be suspicious. Could we just wait until a little later tonight?"

"It's now or never, Vanja," Evgen said.

"Just give me a few hours."

"Fine. One o'clock."

Evgen turned around and walked into Amatka, shoulders pulled up to his ears. He looked small against the plant-house wall.

Nina came down into the kitchen and ate the fried porridge Vanja served. She moved slowly as though she were in pain, but at least she ate. They didn't talk. When Nina had managed a little more than half of her portion, she got up and put the plate in the fridge. Then she kissed the top of Vanja's head and went upstairs. When Vanja came up a while later, she'd gone back to bed. Her own, this time.

Vanja went into her own room, closed the door, and sat down at her desk. She took the thing that had been a pencil out of her pocket and studied it. It still had the same approximate shape she'd managed to impose on it earlier. The whitish surface was cool and a little rough. She rolled it between her thumb and forefinger. "Spoon," she whispered. "Spoon, spoon, spoon, spoon, spoon."

A tiny shudder went through the material. Her marking pen lay next to the typewriter. She uncorked it and wrote SPOON. The tip of her pen punched through the surface in a couple of spots; it felt a lot like sticking a fork in a mushroom. Vanja leaned forward over the table. She closed her eyes and tried to make herself do that thing with her mind, that shameful thing, to truly imagine that a thing was something other than it was. "Spoon," she breathed. "Spoon, spoon, spoon, spoon, spoon-spoon-spoon-spoon-spoon-spoon—"

She was close enough to hear the wet noise of the substance shifting, and she opened her eyes. One of the ends had flattened into a concave disc. It looked like a spoon, sort of. She took a deep breath and tried again.

After an hour and a half, she had managed to create something that actually looked like a real spoon, albeit transparent, rough, and a little dented. The effort had made her head feel empty. Still, she had found the way that seemed to work best: to use speech, writing, and thought to describe in detail something that didn't exist, to make it come into existence. At first it had made her nauseous, but then the pit of her stomach had begun to tingle.

Vanja resisted the temptation to try to create something bigger. She wrapped the spoon in a sock and stuffed it into the pocket of her anorak. It was late. She got undressed, went into Nina's room, and crawled into bed. Nina wrapped an arm around her. She would just lie here until Nina was deep asleep, then go to meet Evgen.

She fell asleep instantly.

THIRDAY

Vanja woke with a start to the breaking of the ice. How long had Evgen waited for her? Was he angry? Had he gone without her? There was no way for her to check until after work.

Nina was frying root vegetables in the kitchen. Her eyes were swollen but she was dressed and had made an attempt to untangle her curls. Vanja wrapped her arms around her and rested her cheek against her back, listening to the air rushing in and out of her lungs.

"Slept okay?" Nina's voice vibrated against her cheek.

"Fine. And you?"

"Great. Hey, would you check if Ulla wants breakfast?"

Vanja frowned. "When was the last time you saw her?"

"I thought you knew."

Vanja let go of Nina. "Not since . . . not for days."

"Why haven't we . . ."

They started for the stairs as one.

There was no reply when Nina knocked on Ulla's door. She pushed the handle down, but the door wouldn't budge. She ran up to her own room to get the spare key. Vanja put her ear to the door, but couldn't hear anything on the other side. When Nina finally found the spare key and got the door open, they were met by silence. Nina went inside and shrunk back from something before Vanja had time to see what it was. She backed into the door on the right.

Now that Nina wasn't blocking the view, Vanja could see into the room straight ahead, Ulla's room. The door was wide open. In the light falling in through the window, the substance flowing out of the room shimmered yellow. Nina let out a breath that sounded more like a groan, turned around, and opened the door behind her. Then she crossed the corridor on stiff legs and opened the door to the left. After looking inside, she turned to the first room and leaned over to see inside. She turned back to Vanja. Her face had taken on a greenish hue.

"Ulla isn't here. I'll go get cleaners." She pushed past Vanja and ran down the stairs three steps at a time.

Vanja stayed in the doorway. The mess before her no longer inspired the same terror. She walked over to it, crouched down, and gingerly put a hand on its gelatinous surface. It was warm, body temperature, and buzzed under her hand, twitching almost. She rose and craned her neck to look inside the room. Ulla wasn't there. Neither was the furniture. But on top of a quivering, transparent mound rested a box she recognized. The last time she'd seen it was in Evgen's hands, in old Amatka. The outer and inner lids had been removed. The box was still brimming with papers—the letters, the logs that told the true story of Amatka's past. Ulla must have shadowed Vanja and Evgen to old Amatka and taken them.

The other rooms were empty. Vanja returned to the corridor and for a moment considered wading into the mess and grabbing as many papers as she could. If she took her boots off, she might be able to do it. She was unlacing one of them when she caught the sound of Nina coming back up the stairs. Vanja hastily retreated to the hallway.

"They're on their way," Nina said from the landing. "They're coming. Shut the door."

She bent over, panting, her hands on her knees. She didn't seem to notice Vanja's unlaced boot.

"Ulla isn't there," Vanja said, pointlessly.

Nina nodded. "Nope. We'll have to report her missing."

"I will," Vanja replied.

She pulled her anorak on and left. The papers would have to stay where they were. There was no way she could sneak them past Nina.

Outside, an acrid stink filled the air. A pillar of grayish-black smoke rose toward the sky to the north. There were residential houses in northern Amatka, plant houses. And the library. The closer Vanja came to the pillar of smoke, the more citizens hurried down the street, all heading north.

When Vanja finally arrived, there was no doubt about it: the library was on fire. There were no flames, just thick black smoke billowing out through the broken windows. Part of the crowd had gathered around an old man leaning on a walker. He was holding forth in a deep and penetrating voice.

". . . fetched the librarian," he said as Vanja came closer. "I saw the whole thing. He came running out of the library and then it was on fire. And he lay down in the street and coughed. And laughed! He was laughing! Then the rescue workers came and took him. I told them what I'd seen. He started the fire himself, I'm telling you."

His audience was mumbling to one another. "What happened?" someone at the back asked. "The librarian set it on fire!" someone else replied.

The old man started over. "I saw the whole thing," he intoned. "It's all ablaze. Nothing left in there."

"Did he say anything?" Vanja asked.

"What?" The man turned his head.

"Did he say anything," Vanja repeated.

"Oh, yes, but it was just nonsense," the man said. "He said, 'We'll all be free.'"

Vanja turned around and forced herself to walk to the office at a normal pace. She breathed in, counted to three, breathed out, counted to three, breathed in. It didn't help much.

———

The reception was crowded. Several couriers were heading out; at the reception desk, Anders was deep in intense conversation with what looked like two high-ranking administrators. One of them followed him in behind the counter and into the archive.

"What's going on?" Vanja asked the administrator who had stayed at the counter and was drumming his fingers against the gray surface.

The administrator studied Vanja. "What's your security level?"

"I'm not sure. I'm the reception assistant," Vanja replied hesitantly.

"If you don't know what your security level is, it's not high enough." The administrator graced her with a tight-lipped smile and resumed drumming on the desk. "Don't you have work to do?"

On the third floor, in the department of civil affairs, there was an air of subdued but frantic activity. When Vanja came in to report Ulla's disappearance, she was handed a stack of blank forms. The bloated clerk kept fiddling with his beard and glowered at Vanja across his desk when she couldn't say how long Ulla had been missing, even though they lived in the same household. He shook his head and flipped through a binder, looking for yet another form.

"I'll have to make a separate report of this," he said, and took out a pencil. "Neglect of housemate. Names of the other occupants?"

"Neglect of housemate?" Vanja put her pencil down. "I don't understand."

"Here, in Amatka," the clerk intoned, "whoever has a housemate with special needs, be it physical or mental, must ascertain daily that said housemate is in good health and having their needs met." He looked at Vanja, his upper lip curling into a sneer. "Maybe you don't do that in Essre, but here we take solidarity very seriously. It is your responsibility to acquaint yourself with the rules."

"My apologies," Vanja said. "There were circumstances. One of our other housemates died."

"Were you close?"

"No."

"Then why didn't you have the presence of mind to visit poor Ulla?"

Vanja squirmed. "I forgot. I was taking care of Nina. A housemate. She was close to him."

"Close to whom?"

"To Ivar. The man who died."

"That's all very well." The clerk started filling out his own form. "There will be an investigation."

When Vanja had completed her forms, the clerk skimmed through them, nodded, and sent her to the office next door. Next door, they took the forms for registration and forwarding to the police department. Vanja was told to return to work and go about her business as usual. They made her file a copy of her own report.

The rest of the day dragged. The buzzing noise, which until now had mostly felt like a vibration, came within her range of hearing as a deep bass note resonating in the background. If anyone else heard it, they didn't mention it.

Every time someone walked past the reception, Vanja half expected them to stop and tell her that Evgen was dead, that Evgen had reported her, that they'd found Ulla's body, that they'd found the papers in Ulla's room, that Nina and Vanja were to be arrested on account of the papers. But each time, it turned out to be something else, and she breathed a bit more easily. The visitors looked harassed and tense. Anders's virtually cheerful mood from yesterday had mutated into a kind of grim hysteria. He accompanied administrators to the archive and watched them come out again carrying sturdy boxes Vanja had never seen before, which must have come from the secure archive. She refrained from asking. It felt safer to go unnoticed.

In the afternoon, the same clerk who had taken Vanja's report came downstairs and handed a form over to Anders. "They've arrested that librarian now," he said.

Anders brightened. "Have they, now!"

The clerk nodded and ran his fingers through his beard. "Yep."

Vanja tried to look suitably interested. "What will happen to him?"

The clerk peered at Vanja and then at Anders. "He'll be interrogated. I suppose the next step is finding out whether he was acting alone or not." He went back to combing his beard.

On the plaza around the commune office people walked with drawn-up shoulders and frequent glances toward the horizon. A couple of them just stood there, staring. Vanja followed their eyes. They were all looking eastward, in the direction of the lake. Beyond the low houses of the colony, a narrow silhouette rose toward the sky. It was curved at the end. It seemed to grow taller by the minute. Somewhere in the plaza, someone let out a shrill noise that went on and on. The rest of the colony had discovered the pipes.

FOURDAY

The children were sent away on Fourday morning. They were packed into the passenger car, the freight cars, the locomotive, the youngest children in the arms of the older. A huddle of parents who couldn't let their children go without saying good-bye waited on the platform. They couldn't touch them, just watch. Many of them tried to smile and look proud. Some called out, wishing the children an exciting trip, telling them to behave. Nina stood at the edge of the group. She was hugging herself, clutching Vanja's hand hard enough to make it painful. Tora and Ida were nowhere to be seen; they had been among the first to get on the train. The last of the children were climbing up the stairs now, each with a small satchel slung across his or her shoulder.

A man left the group and rushed over to a blond boy who stood in line to board the passenger car. He picked the boy up and held him close. Over the boy's shoulder, Vanja could see his father's face contorting in pain, his teeth bared. She had to look away.

In the shocked silence that descended on the platform, the only sound was the man's hacking sobs. Eventually, a platform worker took him by the shoulder—not unkindly—and pried the boy out of his arms. The father stood with his hands outstretched while the boy was lifted onto the train. The last door closed with a crash that reverberated down the platform. Nina winced, as though she had been struck. She turned around and walked back into the colony, her strides so long Vanja had to follow at a trot.

Through couriers and overseers, the committee saw to it that everyone remembered that sending the children away was just a safety precaution. After all, this had been done before, on occasion, just in case. Every time, the children had been allowed to return within a week.

Vanja was asked to telephone Essre to inform them about the children's imminent arrival. The person on the other end sounded bewildered.

"You're breaking up," he said. "What's that?"

"We're sending the children," Vanja repeated.

"I can't hear you properly," said the operator. "If there are more of you, please take turns speaking."

"It's just me," Vanja said.

"I'm hanging up now," the operator said. "I'll try calling you up."

The telephone went dead. Vanja waited for the call for fifteen minutes before trying herself. There was only the hiss of an empty line.

Paint and brushes were distributed at midday, to supplement verbal marking with text. Anders sent Vanja out to mark corridor walls, doors, and stairs. The departments were all buzzing with quietly frantic activity: hurried steps across office floors, agitated voices behind closed doors. Occasionally someone would open a door to peer suspiciously down the corridor where Vanja was marking a wall or a staircase. She tried to make out the conversations but was only able to catch random words here and there, none of which made her any the wiser. The black paint had an overpowering smell and wouldn't quite stick to the walls; it took two layers to make the letters solid. When

Vanja finally ran out of paint, her shoulder hurt and her right hand was cramping. She just made it back in time for the three o'clock marking in the reception.

The line to the leisure center wound all the way into the street. Everyone was on time and waited in line in silence. Nina looked pale and somehow shorter than usual. She clutched Vanja's hand tightly.

Vanja had come home from work to find Nina in the kitchen with a pair of administrators. One of them had led Nina outside; the other had asked Vanja to sit down. The administrators had seemed stressed and distracted. They asked only a handful of questions: when Ulla was last seen, if Vanja had been into Ulla's room (once), if she had noticed this one box on that occasion (no), if she knew whether Ulla harbored subversive opinions (no), if it was her opinion that Ulla might be senile (yes, maybe). They had soon made to leave, parting with an explicit promise to return.

"Where's the next one?" one of them had asked the other as the front door closed behind them.

Vanja had gone upstairs. The door to Ulla's flat was still sealed. Then it had been time for leisure.

When the evening meal, consisting of nothing more than mushroom and bean porridge, had been served and people were busy eating, committee member Jolas' Greta climbed the dais. She talked about what had happened to the library. Her voice was firm, with an undertone of suppressed anger.

"A citizen has been apprehended. He is a librarian. We have received a confession." Greta paused and looked out at her audience.

Vanja held her breath. What had he told them? Had he mentioned her name? Wouldn't they have arrested her if that were the case? "During the interrogation," Greta continued, "he confessed that he started the fire on purpose. He also admitted that his intention was to undermine the commune by destroying all our good paper."

Greta paused again and looked down at her hands. When she raised her head again, she fixed on each citizen in turn. "We know that this type of act, this way of thinking, could not have . . . come to fruition . . . had not something been amiss in the group as a whole. In a healthy commune, each member safeguards the group. In a healthy commune, the librarian doesn't burn down the library."

Greta smiled wistfully. "This man was lonely. He had no one to talk to, no one to confide in. Loneliness is dangerous. Silence is dangerous. Through loneliness and silence, a small feeling of discontent can grow into illness. If only he had had someone to talk to. If only he had felt part of this community, if he had felt a sense of responsibility toward the commune."

She shook her head. "Looked at this way, we are all to blame for what happened. We must never let our comrades feel alone."

Someone began to clap. The applause spread like thunder through the hall. Greta raised her hands in a calming gesture until the crowd had settled down. "Tonight, we're going to start treating the disease that is loneliness. We are going to talk about our pain, our thoughts, and through this become closer to one another. No one will be angry with you. No one will punish you. Your comrades will greet you with sympathy. Don't be afraid! Come." Greta took a step to the side and made a beckoning gesture.

As if on cue, a young woman stepped up onto the dais. She talked about how she had uncharitable thoughts about her housemates, but it was really because she felt inferior to them. The crowd applauded her. She stepped down from the dais with tears running down her face. She was met by her housemates, who embraced and kissed her.

People were almost launching themselves at the dais after that. Citizens stood up one after the other, shouting their loneliness to the commune, their disloyal thoughts, their petty thefts of office supplies, their unkind deeds toward their fellow comrades. One after the other, they were applauded and embraced by their friends. The atmosphere turned frenzied. The dais wasn't enough. Some stood up on benches and tables to speak to those nearby. Vanja and Nina were still seated, Nina gazing into the distance, her hand in Vanja's a warm, calm spot in the swirling chaos. The hysteria spread to their table. Their neighbors got up to tell everyone about doubt, pettiness, loneliness. They wept as they unburdened themselves of their minor infractions. Eventually a momentary silence descended. The others turned to Vanja and Nina.

"Say something," a man next to them urged.

His face was streaked with salt and tears. He had confessed to once slapping his daughter for being loud on a Sixday.

Vanja's arms and legs went numb. Next to her, Nina gave a start, as if only now realizing where she was. The silence grew longer.

The man with the tear-streaked cheeks took Vanja's free hand and caressed it. "You can tell us."

His hand was clammy against her skin. Disgust drove her across a line she hadn't been aware of.

"I have nothing to confess," she said loudly. "I'm not going to say sorry."

The others stared at her, openmouthed. Vanja pulled free of the man's grip. She took a clumsy step backward over the bench. Nina was still holding her other hand. She looked up at Vanja with something like horror.

"I haven't done anything wrong," Vanja told her. "I haven't."

Nina didn't try to hold her back. Vanja pushed through the ecstatic crowd, out into the damp night.

"Wait!"

It was Nina. The rec center's doors swung shut behind her. They were alone in the street, bathed in the murmur from the hall. Nina raised her hands and let them fall back down. She came close enough to put a hand on Vanja's shoulder. "Where are you going?"

Vanja looked at the hand on her shoulder, her eyes tracing the length of the arm to Nina's shoulder and face. Nina's features had become hollow, gaunt. The solid security that Vanja had curled up against was no longer there. "I'm going home," she replied.

Nina's eyes welled up. Her chin trembled. "No you're not. You're a lousy liar."

"I'm not going to sit in there and tell them I did something wrong. I've always had to do that, and I'm tired of it." That part at least was true.

"Look, Vanja, everyone makes mistakes. That's why we're in there right now—not to point fingers, but to acknowledge that we all make mistakes sometimes so that we don't have to feel like we're the only ones. . . ."

"Sometimes! It's wonderful how you only make mistakes sometimes, isn't it! Big and strong and healthy and two children and saving lives every day, but sometimes things go a little awry. It must be nice to go and have a nice little confession, then, so you can go home and feel pleased about being such a good girl."

Nina had clapped a hand over her mouth. She took a couple of steps back, frowning. Vanja realized that she might have been yelling. It didn't matter.

Vanja tapped her own chest. "But what about me. I'm nothing but wrong. I'm supposed to go inside and be sorry about it?" Vanja shook her head. "Go inside and do some confessing if it makes you feel better. I'm done."

Nina was quiet for a long moment. "I understand." Her voice was small. "So. Are you going home?"

Vanja was silent.

Nina swallowed and blinked several times. "I'll leave you alone."

She turned and walked back toward the leisure center. Shouts and cries poured into the street when she opened the doors and stepped inside.

Vanja set off westward. She slowed down when she passed Leisure Center Three. Two couriers in gray overalls were exiting, holding a woman who seemed to be struggling to break free.

"But we were supposed to tell!" she said, despair in her voice. "It was supposed to be good for us!" Her eyes locked on Vanja's. "Hey, you! Can't you see what they're doing?"

The couriers halted and turned toward Vanja. "Go home," one of them said. "Now."

Vanja kept walking, her eyes on the ground in front of her. The arrested woman called after her until her voice was suddenly cut off.

Vanja stayed close to the walls, forcing herself to walk at a normal pace. She slipped into a side street whenever she spotted other pedestrians. Once, she encountered another pair of couriers escorting a citizen between them. Vanja walked over to a nearby residential building and pretended to be busy scraping dirt off her shoes.

When she finally reached the plant-house ring, it was deserted. The plant-house lamps were lit, but no night growers cast shadows on the walls. The first pipe loomed about fifty meters beyond the plant houses, faintly illuminated by the domes. Its angled top end cut a sharp silhouette against the dark gray of the night sky. Vanja halted by the outer edge of the plant-house ring. Snatches of song drifted through the streets behind her, along with cries of anger, drunkenness, or fear. The breeze coming in from the tundra smelled of wet grass and old vehicles. The sight of the impossibly huge pipes made it hard to breathe, hard to take the first step. Instinct shrieked at her to run before it was too late, run and go to ground, hide in a faraway corner, under a bed, in Nina's arms, be quiet and invisible until the pipes moved elsewhere. But there were no safe places anymore. The only way was onward. She forced her feet forward, step by step, toward the pipe that led down to the machine.

When she finally found the right spot, she had come out on the other side of fear. Her skin felt stretched and prickly, her legs soft and unsteady, but it was like looking out a window. She was inside, her body and the tundra outside. The low opening was still there. The ladder was still attached to the inside. Resting her hand on the edge, she realized she hadn't brought a flashlight. She would have to do this in the dark. Terror came creeping back.

"It's only my body doing this," Vanja whispered to herself. "It's not me. It's only my body." She swung a leg over the rim.

The weak light from above faded almost immediately. When she finally set her foot on firm ground, the darkness was complete, aside from the colorful trails and blotches her brain created to fill the absence of light. The vibration was stronger here, the noise clear and suddenly complex; it wasn't a single buzzing, but the sound of many small parts working in unison. She wasn't alone in the tunnel. Something else was in there with her. Vanja stood still, waiting while bile rose in her throat. Nothing happened. There was only the awareness of a vast presence. She walked slowly toward the sound, sticking closely to the rough wall.

Her left foot hit the door with a crash that made her crouch against the wall and shield her head with her arms. In the echo that followed, she thought she could hear small, quick footsteps down the tunnel. She reached up and fumbled for the handle. It allowed itself to be pushed down. She slunk in through the opening and closed the door as quickly as she could without making a racket.

On the other side, the greenish-white lichen that dotted the ceiling beat the darkness into retreat and illuminated the staircase. Vanja sat on the steps until she no longer had to struggle to breathe, then continued down, to the door that waited at the bottom. When she opened it, the noise suddenly swelled to a deafening roar.

The air was damp and heavy with a stench of salt and sewage that stuck to the roof of her mouth. The machine working in the middle of the room seemed to have grown. The wheel had cut a deep furrow in the chamber's ceiling. Shards and chipped stone littered the ground around the engine, which looked more rounded somehow. Someone was standing in front of the machine, watching Vanja.

Vanja's eyes slipped when she tried to focus on whoever it was. It was a person, but what features or coloring or shape they had was impossible to tell. It was neither, indeterminate, not entirely there. Vanja had to avert her eyes. At the edge of her vision, she could see the shape approach. Looking indirectly seemed fruitful: she could make out an eye, hands that weren't entirely hands, skin, but everything kept flowing and shifting. She knew who it had to be and took a deep and shaky breath.

"Are you Berols' Anna?"

The figure paused. "Are you Berols' Anna?" Its voice vibrated through Vanja's chest. "Are you?"

"Are you?"

Laughter. "Are you are you?"

It came closer. Heat radiated from its mass. Something soft touched Vanja's cheek, tracing the contours of her face. "Are you?" It no longer sounded like mimicry. A short pause. "Yes. Also."

"Did you build the machine? And the tunnels? And the pipes? What does the machine do?" Vanja asked.

"Everyone built. We and you. The machine is ours." The thing caressing Vanja's face suddenly pinched her cheek. "You thought it. We thought it."

Vanja tried to focus on Berols' Anna's shape again, only to be rewarded with a twinge of pain between her eyes. "Are you happy?" she asked. "Are you a happy commune?"

Berols' Anna laughed again. "The word . . . the language. Is too small. Yes. We are everything. But you"—a soft touch against her cheek again—"you are not."

"Happy? Or too small?"

Warmth twined itself around Vanja's body. A heavy scent of something like blood crowded out the stench of sewage. The heat made her fear dissipate. "Yes," Berols' Anna murmured above her. "Wan-ja. Your shell is too small."

Vanja grasped what felt like an arm. It was solid, yet not. It buzzed with restrained energy. "Can you come and save us? In Amatka?"

"Let us in," Berols' Anna crooned.

"But how?"

"Remove the names. Set the words free. Just a little more. Burn a little more."

"Like the library."

"Yes. A little more."

"Then you'll come?"

"Then we'll come. You'll be everything. You'll all be everything."

Berols' Anna grazed Vanja's cheek and raised her chin. Vanja opened her eyes and looked into Berols' Anna's face, and it suddenly snapped into focus.

The night after Lars had told her about the lights in the sky above the old world, Vanja had had a dream. The gray veil that enshrouded the sky had cracked and blown away. Against a deep black background, gigantic spheres, glowing in colors Vanja had never seen before, slowly moved through the heavens with a sound that shook the earth. The ground fell away beneath her. She hung suspended in the void, inconceivably small amid the glory of the spheres.

That same feeling returned when she looked into Berols' Anna's eyes. It blew everything else away.

Vanja didn't know how much time had passed since she'd climbed down the shaft, but it was still late evening or night when she came back up. The pipes rising into the sky no longer terrified her. They belonged to Amatka. All around her was the low creaking of new pipes pushing out of the ground.

The streets were empty. From some houses noise as if from a party or a fight could be heard. The scrap boxes outside the buildings had been knocked over. From one of them a large puddle of gloop had leaked onto the pavement. Somewhere to the east was Nina, swept up in the hysteria.

The door to the commune office was open. Windows were lit here and there in the building, especially on the top floor where the committee was at work. The reception was dark, but when Vanja turned on a desk lamp, it became apparent that someone had been there at some point during the evening. Papers and logs were in disarray, and the door to the archive stood ajar. Downstairs, the sort of inventory lists that were plastered throughout the colony lay scattered on the floor. The door to the secure archive was still closed and locked. It would never open without a key. Vanja stuck her hand into the pocket of her anorak, fingering the coagulated piece of gloop.

There were plenty of marking pens in the reception. Once back down in the archive, Vanja closed the door behind her, took the spoon-shaped lump from her pocket, and wrote KEY on the shaft. "Key, key, key, key, key," she whispered.

It twitched in her hand. Something inside Vanja resisted. Calling a thing by another name still gave rise to a vague, indeterminate horror that made her brain glitch. She gritted her teeth and closed her eyes. "Key, key, key, key. This is a key. I am holding a key in my hand."

When she opened her eyes again, she was holding a stick that branched at one end. Calling it a key was a bit of a stretch. But then, she hadn't given it a lock to open. She pushed the key-thing into the lock on the door to the secure archive. "Key, key, key."

The key-thing let itself sink into the lock. Vanja pushed until she met resistance and closed her eyes again. "The key has cuts that fit the bolts in the lock. The cuts are hard enough to move the bolts. The key fits the lock. The cuts on the bit fit the bolts. The key can open the lock." Her head hurt.

Eventually she opened her eyes again. She tried to turn the stick to the left but lost her grip—the key didn't have a proper bow, after all. Vanja screwed her eyes shut. "The key has a bow, the key has a bow, the key has a bow."

The gloop flattened between her fingers and her headache intensified, converging sharply at a point behind her left eye. But she could turn the key now. The bolts rotated with a series of clicks. She pulled the key out again and put it in her pocket. Then she opened the door to the secure archive.

It wasn't much bigger than a bathroom; all it held was a filing cabinet with three drawers. The topmost drawer had a handwritten label that read INCIDENT REPORTS; the other two were labeled HISTORY and RULES AND REGULATIONS. Vanja opened INCIDENT REPORTS. It contained a suspension-file system with folders in receding chronological order. The oldest folders were thin, but the closer they came to the present day, the thicker the files grew. Vanja pulled out the outermost folder and opened the cover. According to a helpful little index, the folder contained one form per incident. The report titles referred to the type of event: *Collapse, Increased Dissolution per Quadrant*, something called *Manifestations*.

One Seconday, someone had seen a train arrive and then vanish from where it was parked on the rails.

A group of children had been playing unapproved games in a corner of Children's House Four. Someone had begun to pretend that one thing was another. Suddenly every single object in the room had dissolved.

There were several cases of people appearing at the edges of the colony. The individuals could not be identified as citizens and "looked strange."

The latest incident report was only a few days old. It concerned the collapse in the mushroom chambers and the subsequent discovery of the pipes. A summary of Ivar's statement was attached to the form. There was no mention of yesterday's events, or the day before that. Maybe they were too busy now to write reports. Vanja leafed back through the years. The same types of events occurred again and again.

At the far back, a folder containing a stapled bundle of papers. The title read *Fish in Balbit*. The reports described an event where the first generation of children had started playing a new game: they went "fishing." The children had learned about "fish" from the books their parents had brought with them from the old world. Previous investigations had established that ocean life had evolved no further than algae. Even so, the children were pulling "fish" out of the water.

According to the informant, the adults discovered what was going on only when the children, who had been left unsupervised, had pulled a large amount of "fish" out of the water.

The informant states that the things scattered around the children could superficially be said to resemble fish, but upon dissection turned out to have "neither guts nor spine, just some sort of gunk inside." It emerged that the children had organized a competition. The children would take turns announcing the description of the fish they planned to catch and were awarded points according to how much the catch resembled the description.

A decision was made on the spot to confiscate and destroy all books containing pictures and descriptions of marine wildlife. Furthermore, a motion will be proposed to the Central Administration in Essre for stricter regulation of contents in books available to the public, and to children in particular. This incident is particularly alarming considering the recent events in Colony 5.

Vanja closed the drawer and opened the next one. The files had been shoved in haphazardly, meeting protocols jumbled with what looked like essays and lists. Vanja reached into the very back of the drawer and pulled out one of the oldest folders.

Edict: Name Usage

After the tragic events that lay waste to Sunborough, it is the decision of the Central Administration that all names of places and people in the colonies be regulated, effective immediately. Any name that refers to a thing or animal, is immediately homonymic with a word used to denote another meaning in modern language, or in any other way attributes qualities to the place or person shall be changed to an approved name. Approved names shall be simple and mirror the origin of the majority of the pioneers. All place-names will be replaced with a letter combination chosen at random. New place-names are as follows:

Designation/Old name/New name
Colony 1 / Base / Essre

Colony 2 / Seaview / Balbit

Colony 3 / Oilfield / Odek

Colony 4 / Frostville / Amatka

Colony 5 / Sunborough / —

They had named Colony 5 after a light in the sky, and the world had replied.

Vanja put the papers back into the folder and looked at her wrist clock. It would be morning soon. She couldn't waste the night reading if she were to have any hope of doing what she had come for. She pulled the bottom drawer out and off its tracks. It was so heavy she could barely lift it. She lugged it upstairs to the reception, where she left it under the front desk. She repeated the process with the other two drawers and returned to the main archive.

With all the drawers completely pulled out, the space left in the middle was just big enough to stand in. Vanja looked around. All this paper really only served one purpose: to anchor the colony's shape, to keep people from breaking free. It would burn in no time at all. All she had to do was set fire to it. Set fire to it and scatter the secure archive in the streets. Then she would tell them. She would tell them all. People had a right to know how trapped they were, how much they had never been allowed to know, how they had never been allowed to choose what life they wanted to live.

Vanja abruptly realized she had nothing to light the paper with. She had never even owned a lighter. Evgen had had one, not she. She drummed her hands on her thighs in frustration. "Come on, burn," she hissed at the archive. "Burn."

A few of the papers rustled as if in a breeze. Of course. Vanja let out a laugh. She pulled a bundle of mycopaper out of the closest drawer and stared at it. "You're burning," she told the paper. "You're burning, burning, burning."

When the mycopaper flared up, it was so sudden it scorched her fingertips and made her drop it. It landed in a box of mixed good and mycopaper. The good paper wasn't immune to the flames. It almost burned better than the mycopaper. Vanja took papers from the other drawers, lit them and put them back, until half of the archive was ablaze and the flames were spreading rapidly on their own. Black smoke roiled up toward the ceiling, choking her. She crawled up the stairs on her hands and knees.

They were waiting for her at the front desk. A clerk was crouched by the drawers from the secure archive, going through the folders. Two sturdy couriers were on their way through the reception toward the archive door. They stepped back as Vanja threw the door open and smoke poured out.

"There she is!" the clerk yelled.

Two shoulders slammed into Vanja's ribs as the couriers both tackled her.

The sky was brightening as they led Vanja through the streets. One of the couriers had landed a blow on the side of her head. Her field of vision had darkened for a moment, and after that it was hard to think properly. Moving her head hurt.

The noise that cut through the air was low at first, then rose in pitch and volume, then fell again, up and down. Vanja and her captors all looked up. All around the colony, pipes loomed against the sky. They were wailing.

FIFDAY

It could have been any office: a desk with a notepad, one chair behind the desk, another in front of it. A few inspirational posters on the wall. Behind the desk sat a middle-aged man in rumpled overalls. His hair was a little too long, his beard slightly unkempt; it made him seem absent-minded in a friendly way. Vanja had been gagged. It happened after her head cleared up and she had tried—and almost succeeded—to set fire to one of the couriers' overalls. In response, they had gagged her and tied her hands behind her back. The gag chafed at the corners of her mouth. The restraints cut into her wrists. Leaning back on the chair put an unpleasant strain on her shoulders. The fatigue and excitement had made her shaky and cold, and her vision wavered. When she shifted in the chair, a heavy hand landed on her shoulder, holding her still.

The man folded his hands on the desk in front of him and studied Vanja. He gave her a sad smile. "Brilars' Vanja Essre Two. That's you, isn't it?"

Vanja glared at him.

The man sighed quietly. "No, you don't have to try to answer. I know it's you. Brilars' Vanja Essre Two, recently arrived from Essre to conduct market research. You met a woman, quit your job, and settled here. So far, so good. But now you've lost your way. Well." He held out his hands, palms up. "Allow me to introduce myself. My name is Ladis' Harri. I'm the speaker of Amatka's committee. First of all, Vanja, I have to inform you that you've been arrested for destruction of public property, endangering the public, and subversive activity. And I feel it's important that you and I have a conversation about what happened. I would like to know how all this came to pass."

Harri stood up and leaned across the desk. He smelled faintly of coffee and liquor. "I'm thinking I might take the gag off, Vanja. Otherwise it'll be hard for us to talk. But I have to be sure you won't do anything foolish. Leila is standing right behind you, and she'll sedate you if you do. And that would be a pity, because I would really like to talk to you. Can you promise me that we can talk in a calm and collected manner?"

Vanja nodded. Harri smiled and gave the courier behind her a nod. The gag came off, and the pressure around her head eased. Vanja grimaced and licked the corners of her mouth.

Harri leaned back in his chair. "Well, then. So, Vanja. Were you working with someone?"

Vanja shook her head.

Harri nodded slowly. "I should tell you that Nina was the one who reported you."

His words sank into the pit of her stomach.

"She came to us last night, after you disappeared," he continued. "She told us everything. It wasn't easy for her, you know. She really does love you. She said that you've displayed subversive tendencies, but that she'd been hoping you'd come to your senses. And then yesterday you absconded from the leisure center. You told her you were going home?" He pulled out a drawer and took out a thermos and two mugs. "Nina went home to make up with you. Of course, you weren't there. Instead, she found your notes."

Vanja gasped. Harri paused and looked at her. "That's right," he said. "So she decided to do what she thought was best for everyone. And that's what you and I are going to talk about. Doing what's best for everyone. Coffee?"

Vanja declined to answer and looked away. Harri looked a little hurt. He unscrewed the lid and poured himself a cup. "We have something of an emergency on our hands." He sipped the coffee. The hand holding the cup shook a little. "In light of that, I'll have to keep this short. We know most of it already: you've intentionally let objects in your home dissolve; you've been conspiring with the librarian Samins' Evgen. . . ."

Harri nodded when Vanja gave a start. "Yes, he confessed, too. He didn't mention you, but Nina knew that the two of you were friends. And then there's what we've gleaned from your notes—that you've been conspiring with Sarols' Ulla, and that you've studied subversive documents she kept in her room. We found the box. Ulla sold you out, Vanja."

When Vanja opened her mouth to protest, he held up a hand. With the other, he opened the notebook. "I quote: '. . . that I know exactly how things really are and still claim that E.H.S.'s products are made of something else. Calls the cup a knife. U. refers to the bag and that I wanted it to dissolve because I'm unhappy with the order of things.' Do you deny that you wrote this? No?" He leaned forward. "And as we know, it doesn't end there. You've been outside the colony, and you've approached quarantined areas. And finally this. Looting the archive and exposing sensitive documents." He leaned back. "That someone would do these things . . . it makes me so sad."

He seemed to be waiting for an answer. Vanja couldn't summon the strength to speak.

Harri shook his head. "You're not the first to foment rebellion."

Vanja could hear the quotation marks around the last word. "The powers that be, we're tyrants, right? It's oppression, right?" He tilted his head to catch Vanja's eye. "Right?"

"Yes," Vanja managed. It came out as an "uh."

"You know how this place works. Everyone does. We're a finite population in a world we don't really understand. We struggle endlessly to maintain order. That struggle entails a society with strict rules."

Harri turned the cup in his hands. "What's less widely known is that we have nowhere else to go, Vanja. We can't go back. The way is shut. Our only choice is to either follow the rules or be destroyed." His eyes were welling up. "People will die because of what you've done, Vanja. People have already died."

"We're already dead." Vanja forced the words out between dry lips. "This is no life. You've taken it."

Harri raised his eyebrows. "Who do you mean by 'you,' Vanja? The committee is elected by the people. The committee is the people. We can be deposed at any time. Anyone can stand in the election. You've voted, haven't you? Maybe you've even been a candidate?"

Vanja squeezed her mouth shut.

Harri sighed and got out of his chair again. "I'm given to understand that you've led a difficult life, Vanja. You're angry and disappointed. We've all agreed on a set of rules necessary for our survival, but some people just can't live by them. You're raging against a system you feel protects the group but hurts you. So you've decided to overthrow the system and let the group perish. Have I got that right?"

Harri waited for a moment. When Vanja didn't reply, he raised his voice. "You're not very chatty, are you? Is this fair, d'you think? To let innocent citizens pay? If that isn't taking someone's life, I don't know what is. Putting yourself above what the people have decided. Have you really nothing to say about that?"

Vanja drew a deep breath. "But that's not how it is. People are unhappy. . . ."

"You are unhappy. And you're alone now. Your coconspirators have left you behind."

A low rumble outside made them both jump. Harri got hold of himself. "Well, then. We're out of time. I'm sorry about what has to happen now, but that's just how it is. You've left us no choice."

There was a stinging pain in her arm. "Berols' Anna," Vanja said. Pressure was spreading through her chest, making it hard to breathe. Her field of vision began to flicker and narrow. Through the haze, she saw the speaker lean in, his eyes widened. "Berols' Anna is coming."

"Keep her sedated until it's done," Ladis' Harri said from far away.

LATER

The bed was comfortable. The pillow was so soft against Vanja's cheek. The blankets were warm and snuggly, and someone had dressed her in soft sleep clothes. She considered getting up but abandoned the thought. She was warm. She hadn't been warm for such a long time. Even her toes and the tip of her nose were warm.

Vanja was a little girl. Lars put his arms around her, and she burrowed her face into his shoulder. He smelled of soil and coffee and beard.

"I missed you," she told him. "I missed you, too," he said.

She drew away and looked at him. His temples were covered in black scabs. "They got you."

He nodded gravely. "So they did."

"I understand now," Vanja said. "We don't know where we are."

"Good girl," Lars said, and patted her cheek. "Good girl."

Two voices were talking to each other above her head. She tried looking at the speakers but couldn't seem to focus her eyes.

"Could you please be quick about it," the lower voice said. "I have somewhere to be."

"Calm down," an older, higher voice replied. "It'll take as long as it takes."

Something tightened above Vanja's left elbow. A couple of fingers tapped at the crook of her arm.

"I can't find a vein," the high voice said.

"I heard the whole first quadrant locked themselves in the mushroom chambers," the low voice said. "But no one issued an order for that, did they?"

A sigh. The pressure around her left arm eased. "No."

A tightening above the right elbow. Tap, tap at the crook of her arm. "There we go. No, there was no order. I guess the first quadrant panicked."

"But why aren't we heading down there? Why are we standing around in here? Everything's going crazy."

A wet cold grazed the inside of Vanja's arm. "Because the mushroom farm isn't safe. If we're going anywhere, it's to the commune office. And besides, hiding isn't exactly sensible. If everyone hides, we have no defense. Amatka is here because we are."

A sharp prick of pain sank into Vanja's skin.

Vanja was a girl again. She was standing on the ice. Daylight fell across the lake, but the ice lay clear and black under her feet. Lars stood a couple of feet away, a little smile on his face.

"Let me show you something," he said.

He stepped behind her, then took her head between his hands and pressed his thumbs against her temples. "Look up, Vanja. Look at the sky."

The clouds drew aside. The sky opened. The light was unbearably bright.

Someone came into the room and gave her water. Her head hurt. She forced her eyes open, but they wouldn't focus. Her eyelids closed again. She said something, and a hand lightly stroked her forehead in response. She asked where she was. The hand patted her on the shoulder and straightened her blankets.

A warm hand on hers. "Vanja?"

Fingers weaving themselves with her own. "Vanja, it's Nina. Can you hear me?"

Vanja turned her head. It hurt. She said something.

"I'm so sorry, Vanja," Nina said. "I'm so sorry. I did what I thought was right."

It's all right, Vanja tried to say, *I'm all right*. A noise came out, something that was not what she had wanted to say.

"Let's give it some time," Nina said. "You'll be fine. You'll be fine."

Cool lips on her cheek.

"I have to go," Nina said. "They don't know I'm here. I'll be back."

A voice Vanja recognized, a man's voice. Someone leaning in close. The smell of coffee and liquor. "What's her condition?"

A woman's voice: "The procedure was successful. It's still early on, but she's shown signs of aphasia. What type of aphasia remains to be seen, but it's clear that she can't form words."

"Good."

"Why is she so important, Harri?"

"I'm not at liberty to tell you that. Only that it's very, very important that she doesn't speak."

"Well, we've made sure of that."

"Very good."

"What's really happening out there?"

"We need to stay strong," Harri replied. "Let me know if there's any change in her condition."

"Will do."

Ladis' Harri's presence disappeared. Vanja managed to open her eyes. A woman's face swam into view, a very young nurse. "Can you hear me?" she said.

Vanja replied. "It's all right," the nurse said. "Just nod or shake your head for yes and no. Do you understand?"

Vanja nodded. "Do you understand what happened to you, Vanja?"

Vanja nodded again, slowly.

The nurse reached out and wiped her cheek. "I'm so sorry. Please don't cry. I don't know why they did this to you. I just do the after-care. I have to go. Something's happening out there."

The nurse left. Vanja heard the sound of a key being turned in a lock.

There was a window on the left side of the bed. Darkness was falling. No one came to turn any lights on in her room. The sound of running feet and a murmur of voices came through the window. Vanja turned on her side. Her pillow was so soft her whole face sank into it. She could glimpse a piece of sky through the upper-right corner of her window. Little lights scurried back and forth up there. She watched them until her eyes fell shut again.

Vanja stood on the tundra. Ulla stood in front of her. Her funnel rested against her shoulder and her hair was sprinkled with frost. She looked at Vanja and nodded.

"It's done," she said. "Anna is coming."

Clamoring could be heard from outside: short and long shouts; rumbling, mechanical shrieks. Vanja listened to them for a while. She had to pee. No one came to give her a bottle or a bedpan. Eventually her belly began to hurt. She sat up. When her vision cleared, she could see her legs stretch out from her body in a bed with three blankets. To the left there was a wall with a window, at the foot of the bed another wall. On the right stood a little table, and beyond the table there was a wall with a closed door. A pitcher of water stood on the table. Vanja reached for the pitcher with her right hand, but her fingers wouldn't close around the handle. After a couple of failed attempts, she grabbed it with her left hand instead. The water was tepid and sweet. Some of it trickled out the right corner of her mouth. She put the pitcher back and took three shaky steps toward the door. Her legs were fairly steady, although the right foot dragged a little. She couldn't get the door handle to budge.

She took the pitcher and set it down on the floor, fumbled her pants down to her knees, and crouched. The commotion outside continued unabated. She pulled her pants back up and crawled onto the bed. Sirens began to wail. She couldn't keep her eyes open.

A banging noise on the door. "Vanja! Vanja!"

More banging.

Was that Nina? It was Nina. Why didn't she come in?

"Vanja? Vanja! It's Nina. We're evacuating to the commune office. I'll come get you soon. I love you, Vanja. I don't care what you did. I'm not leaving you here." The voice broke and paused. "I don't have the keys, but I'll come back when it's your turn, it'll be your turn soon. I promise."

Vanja woke up. She looked out the window, and for the first time, properly outside. The commune office towered in the middle of the plaza, angular and solid. Faces looked out from the windows. People were running over the plaza toward the tower. Patients in white robes were walking, hobbling, and rolling out through the hospital doors below. Above them all, pipes towered. Darkness seeped out of their curved mouths, bleeding into the sky. The gray vault was ripped through with dark streaks. Pinpricks of light glowed in the tears.

She sank back into the bed. She was still so tired.

———————

She stood in front of the machine. It was running at full speed, its wheel turning so fast that the spokes were a blur. She could see the pipes now, running away from the machine and into the walls of the cave. The machine glowed with its own light. It made a noise like thunder.

She woke up in front of the window. She didn't know how long she had been sitting there. The sky was dark; a glowing sphere hung in the black, striped in orange and brown. The plaza was deserted. Gaps had appeared in the innermost ring, which had been marked and re-marked with block letters; the pharmacy and the general store were gone. Through the gaps, parts of the residential ring were visible. The lights above the front doors had extended over the street, waving on thin stalks. The doors all stood open.

Vanja's room was high enough that she could see the plant houses at the colony's edge, if that was what they still were. One of them had stretched into a pyramid shape that reflected the light from the thing that sat in the sky. The plant house next to it was moving rest-lessly. As Vanja watched, it shook itself free and rose up in a rain of soil and roots. The windowpane vibrated against Vanja's fingers as the plant house struck out across the tundra on six unsynchronized, rickety legs.

A man came into view, walking from a side street below Vanja's window toward the commune office. He glanced up at the clinic but didn't see her. It was the man who had held Vanja's hand that night in the leisure center, the man who had slapped his daughter. He turned his eyes back toward the plaza, leaning forward as if against a strong wind.

At first it wasn't there, and then it was: a small, half-shaped thing the size of a child, walking next to him. It climbed up the man's trou-ser leg and onto his back, where it wrapped its arms around his neck. Vanja could hear his screams through the window. He fell to his knees and then onto his side before rolling onto his back. The child-shadow straddled his chest. The man's screams had disintegrated into convulsive howls. He banged his head against the ground. After a while he stopped and lay still. The faces watched from the commune office's windows.

Vanja slid off the bed and walked over to the door. She ran her left hand over the surface. She had opened a door without a key once. Thinking was such slow work, but there was a memory: making a key from something else, telling a thing what it should be. The room was empty except for the pitcher, and that was full. She fetched the pillow from the bed. It would have to do. "Aflar," she told the pillow.

She frowned at the word that came out and tried again. *Key.* "Muleg," her mouth said.

Vanja tried again and again. Each time her mouth spurted gibberish. She dropped the pillow and gingerly touched her temple, the shaved spot, the wound. They had taken her words.

The man was still lying prone in the plaza. The child-shape sat on his chest. The man's mouth was moving. It moved quickly at first; he was speaking to the child. Then he shuddered and gasped. Then he spoke again, slowly, and his words sent shockwaves through the air. He took a deep breath and closed his eyes. He lay very still for a moment, like Ivar had, as though he had departed his body.

Eventually as the plant house to the left of the pyramid split down the middle and released a stream of furiously flapping greenery, the man opened his eyes again. He put his arms around the child. It curled up against his chest and sank into his body. Then it was gone. The man stood up on legs that seemed to bend in more than one place. He turned around and staggered off toward the residential ring and its swaying lanterns; he walked into a house and didn't come out again.

Someone jumped from the top floor of the commune office. The ground split open where the body landed. Cracks rushed across the ground and a wedge-shaped section of the plaza fell away without a sound, exposing part of an underground tunnel. Its walls were covered in a pale network of heavy root threads that trembled and shrunk back as daylight rushed in. Round fruiting bodies in shades of faded pink and brown bulged from the mycelium. The fruits swiveled slowly on their short necks, and what might once have been the citizens of the first quadrant raised their white eyes toward the sudden sky.

Vanja remained by the window, watching people jump from the commune office's windows or leave through the front doors and run for the beckoning lanterns of the residential ring. The walls of the commune office had begun to warp, as if buckling under great pressure. The remaining buildings around the plaza were falling in on themselves, one by one. Raw gloop from the dissolved buildings trickled into the exposed mushroom tunnel. The air in the residential and factory rings was turning blue and hazy. Seen through the haze, the low factories and workshops looked wobbly and deformed.

"I'm back," Nina's voice said behind her. "I've come for you."

Nina stood in the doorway of what remained of Vanja's room. The walls beyond the bed and the window had softened, sagging limply from where they were still attached to the ceiling. The door lay crumpled up next to the bed. Vanja hadn't heard it happen.

It was Nina and yet not: she had expanded, as if her body had become too small to contain her. Heat pulsed from her in waves. She carefully enunciated the words one by one, as if speaking was an effort.

"I said I'll come back for you. I've come back for you."

Nina bent down, cradled Vanja's neck in her hand, and pressed her lips against hers. They burned. Blisters formed where their tongues met. She drew back a little.

"Give up or give in," Nina whispered. "I gave in. I gave myself to the world."

Vanja tried to say her name, over and over again. Nina tilted her head, expressions flitting rapidly across her face. Her eyes leaked fluid.

"Don't worry," she said eventually.

Nina took Vanja's hand and led her down the corridor. The floor yielded to their weight; the walls had assumed an oily, slithery shine. Flabby doorways to the left led to rooms where the furniture had dissolved into slime. All empty, except for the last one. Below the window in the last room sat a man with a red beard. Vanja strained to look. The room stank of old excrement, concentrated around Evgen where he huddled, knees drawn up to his chest. He was leaning against the wall, gazing with pale eyes at the sliver of sky that showed through the window. The wound on his temple looked infected. His beard was stiff with dried saliva.

Vanja poked Evgen's shoulder. He didn't react. Nina pulled her back up and led her onward, down to the ground floor. They stepped out of the clinic and into the open space in the middle of what had been Amatka.

To the east, between the undulating ruins of factories and beckoning residences, the view toward the lake was clear. The sky above was robed in black, adorned with brilliantly striped and mottled spheres. On the path from the lake came a crowd; ahead of them strode the being that was Berols' Anna. No one else shone and shimmered like she did. At her side walked Ulla, back straight, eyes gleaming.

Berols' Anna opened her mouth and spoke, and her voice billowed through the air: the voice that had once written the Plant House books, the voice that both mastered matter and belonged to it. She had come to fulfill her promise.

Berols' Anna stopped in front of Vanja where she stood in Nina's embrace. The brightening light from above had not made her features easier to discern; it merely made them glow more strongly than ever. Her eyes mirrored a different landscape than the one they occupied.

"Will you give yourself to the world?"

Anna's voice crashed into Vanja's body like a wave, making her gasp for breath. That's what Vanja was supposed to do. Vanja said it, that she gave herself, that she surrendered, everything she was. A string of syllables dribbled out of her mouth, flat and nonsensical.

Berols' Anna watched Vanja in silence, her hair floating around her like a living thing. After a moment, she grunted. "A person creates the word. Gives in to the world, and becomes the word." It sounded like a sigh. "You have no words. You have been separated."

Separated from her words. The world was built on a new language, and she would not be part of it, only an observer, a watcher.

Berols' Anna turned her head and gazed out on the chaos. "When all of this has become, you will remain; the people like you will remain, all of you, as you are, separate. But we will carry you." She stroked Vanja's cheek. "We will always carry you, little herald."

An observer, a watcher, but beloved. Nina would be with her; Anna would be with her.

Vanja watched as Anna drifted toward the commune office, the only building still standing in the middle of the chaos. It looked out of place, no longer with any meaning, surrounded now by the citizens of Anna's colony. Terrified faces stared out from the windows. Berols' Anna and her people settled down to wait.

Nina and Vanja stayed where they were. They watched from a distance as Berols' Anna and her people sang to the last citizens of Amatka, invited them to take part of the new world or perish with the old. It was something like "The Marking Song," but the words were different; it was a song of making and unmaking, a song not of things that were, but that could be.

Nina folded Vanja into her arms. She still smelled the same. The heat made Vanja drowsy.

She was wrenched from her torpor when Nina stretched and seemed to pull herself together.

"Now," Nina said, "I'm fetching my children from Essre."

She walked out onto the southern part of the plaza. Some kind of communication beyond hearing must have taken place, because from everywhere people came drifting into the plaza. They shone, flew, undulated. They filed out of the colony's ruins, toward the railway in the southwest.

Vanja hung on to Nina's hand. Her right leg wouldn't quite carry her weight, and her bare feet had lost their warmth, but she kept walking. She would walk with them for as long as she could, and when she could walk no more, they would carry her. They all followed the railway south. It thrilled and sang beneath their feet.

ACKNOWLEDGMENTS

This book took a very long time to write. It truly takes a village; so many people have been helpful in the creation of this story.

Special thanks go out to Robin Steen, Lisa Wool-Rim Sjöblom, Nene Ormes, the Word Murderers, and my parents, Göran and Kerstin, for their unwavering support throughout the process. I would also like to thank my Swedish editors, Catharina Wrååk and Titti Persson; Agnes Broome for excellent line editing; my agent, Renée Zuckerbrot; and my editor at Vintage, Tim O'Connell. Finally, to Ann and Jeff Vandermeer: thank you for everything.